NIGHTS IN
BLACK LACE

Also by Noelle Mack

THREE

RED VELVET

JUICY

NIGHTS IN BLACK SATIN

ONE WICKED NIGHT

NIGHTS IN BLACK LEATHER

Published by Kensington Publishing Corporation

NIGHTS IN BLACK LACE

NOELLE MACK

APHRODISIA

KENSINGTON PUBLISHING CORP.
http://www.kensingtonbooks.com

ISBN-13: 978-0-7582-2190-2
ISBN-10: 0-7582-2190-8

First Trade Paperback Printing: October 2008

10 9 8 7 6 5 4 3 2 1

Printed in the United States of America

For JWR—et pourquoi pas

1

"Who is he?"

"I don't know, Odette."

Odette Gaillard looked again at the man seated in the front row next to the catwalk. "He is very handsome."

Her assistant only shrugged. "If you like Americans."

"I do." She shot Marc a laughing look. "And I am in the mood to fall in love."

"Oh, Odette. You should not say that."

"Why not?"

"Because you cannot decide if you are going to fall in love. Love finds you. Then you fall in it."

"Like a mud puddle?" Odette asked.

"Well, sometimes. And sometimes you experience incomparable bliss, accompanied by earth-shattering sex."

Odette gave a snort. "If you are very lucky. I don't think I could describe any love affairs of mine like that. Which doesn't keep me from wanting a new one."

"How long has it been, Odette?"

She answered with vehemence. "Months! The business of fashion has taken over my life!"

Marc waved a hand in a bored way. "Please, spare me the part about you being an artist and how you need to create."

She stuck out her tongue. "I do though."

"And your latest collection is your best yet. Having so many clients is good for you and good for the company."

"Well, the last part is true. We are making millions, Marc. But I still feel very tempted to quit and go do something else."

"What?"

"I don't know."

He sighed deeply. "Putting this show together has unhinged your mind." Marc took another peek at the man his boss had her eye on and shrugged. "But I suppose he would do for a fling."

"Exactly," she said with a feline smile. "Besides, love can last a week or a lifetime. No one knows that at the beginning of an affair."

"*Alors,*" Marc said. "We all wish we did."

Odette stepped away from the curtain that separated the backstage area from the catwalk. "Are you happy that we have a full house?"

"Of course. The dragon lady from *Vogue* is in her accustomed place and we ought to begin."

"I do like peeking at them first," Odette replied. "Especially the celebrities."

"Who is here?" He twitched apart the curtain again. "Aha. Alisa Calderon is making an entrance."

Odette put her cheek next to Marc's to watch a famous Spanish actress saunter to her seat in the front row. "Isn't she going to star in Pedro Almovodar's next movie?"

"I heard that too. You must design something exclusively for her, Odette."

"She is beautiful."

With her cascade of dark hair, doe eyes, huge breasts, and a purse big enough to partly conceal the bodyguard who followed her, the actress caused a stir she seemed to enjoy.

"Beautiful, yes, but she does not know how to accessorize," Marc said disapprovingly. "Her purse is much too large and those shoes do nothing for her legs."

Odette only shrugged. "Since I design neither of those things, that is not my problem. Hmm. I could create a bustier studded with precious stones for her. And if she wears it on the red carpet, then women will be clamoring for their own."

"Fabulously faux, of course."

"Yes, Marc. Great big sparkly fake emeralds and amethysts, I think. With her sultry coloring, perfect. What fun."

Marc thought of something that had evidently been on his mind. "Don't you think that you should move into accessories, Odette?

"Eventually. Ooh, Alisa, you are a naughty girl. How the heads turn when she sits down."

"That is because her skirt hikes up," Marc sniffs. "I can see far more than I want to."

Odette noticed that the American man, whoever he was, did not even look at the actress or seem to notice the hubbub around her. He was talking to a woman next to him, who was delighted to have his attention.

Odette knew her well—Marie Arelquin was a freelance journalist who blogged for *Paris Match*.

"Your friend may have first claim to him," Marc was saying.

Odette pouted. "I have known Marie since our school days. She was never one to share."

"Then you are out of luck," Marc laughed.

The man was laughing at whatever Marie was saying.

"What a nice laugh he has," Odette said, talking to herself

more than to Marc. "I like that type of man. He seems open-minded and open-hearted."

Marc snickered. "And athletic. And too young for you."

"What do you mean by that?" she asked indignantly.

"You will turn thirty in November."

She looked at the man. "He is twenty-seven or twenty-eight. He has smile wrinkles around his eyes."

Marc clutched his clipboard and looked over the top of it. "I suppose so. I would bet he has spent his adolescence on a surfboard. Very bad for the skin."

"And very good for the physical development. Swimmers and surfers have magnificent bodies."

Marc sighed thoughtfully. "Are we reading too much into the fact that he is wearing the top half of a wetsuit?"

"Unzipped," Odette pointed out.

"It is hot out there."

"*He* is hot."

Marc laughed in a low voice. "Ah, Odette, I know you will find a way to meet him before the show is over. But you have only a little while left for this game of peekaboo."

"What time is it?"

Marc looked at his watch, a massive chunk of titanium and black leather and flashing digital functions. "We are a half hour late."

"Excellent. It would not do to be too prompt. I want to whip the audience into a frenzy of longing."

Marc snorted. "Speaking of that, I should go to the dressing room and crack the whip on our models."

"Yes, please see that they have everything they need and that the hairdresser is not being too cruel to them."

"They are such crybabies," Marc sighed. "It's not as if they can do their own styles."

"I want Nadia's hair up in spikes."

He made a note of it.

"And Dabra, in ringlets, but pulled back very tight."

"Could work," he said indifferently, making another note.

"The rest I will leave up to you," Odette said.

"*Merci, madame.*" He gave a mocking little bow and turned to go.

Marc threaded his way through the backstage personnel, stepping carefully over thick lighting cables and avoiding the technicians who swarmed around the area.

Odette looked again through the curtain at the handsome American. Besides the unzipped wetsuit jacket that did very nice things for his broad shoulders, he wore a tank top that fit just right over what she suspected was a beautifully muscled chest. And, *naturellement,* faded jeans. He was perfection.

By her educated guess, the jeans had not been stonewashed or artificially distressed in any way. No, they were molded to his muscular thighs and calves as if he had worn them for months on end in the California sun. Perhaps he was not only a surfer. That taut, sinewy build could just as well be that of a mountaineer.

He might be on his way to Alsace to climb—she could think of no reason for a beach god to be in Paris. Ah, there was another possibility. He could be a cyclist. That would explain the magnificent thighs.

She smiled to herself. An all-around, all-American athlete. Triple A. Exactly what a fling required. Here today and gone tomorrow, always chasing risky new experiences, in love with danger, free as the wind.

In quick succession, she envisioned him shooting the curl of an immense wave, then dangling from a rope in a climber's harness, and finally bent over the handles of a racing bike, legs pumping, his sun-warmed skin bared above the waist. No cologne was more intoxicating than that very masculine smell, as far as she was concerned.

Ah, the pleasures of having an overactive imagination. She felt rather warm herself.

His hair was thick and wavy, also kissed by the sun, its dark brown glinting with an occasional flash of gold under the catwalk's pulsing lights. Odette studied his face. High cheekbones, strong jaw, a deeply carved dimple that flashed when he smiled. And such eyes. Soulful. Expressive. Dark and shadowy. She would have to find a way to meet him somehow, and get a better look close up.

He sat with his legs well apart, and she could not help but notice the other very male characteristics he'd been blessed with under the worn denim. She looked her fill. She doubted that he was wearing underwear. What an animal. His hands were strong and veined, his fingers spread casually open over each solid thigh.

A sensual vision of him with his ragged fly unzipped and his hands around his erect cock came to her mind. She chided herself for having such wayward thoughts only minutes away from the opening of an important show, then forgave herself immediately.

Sexual fantasy was her business, after all. And she had been considering a line of men's underwear to complement the super-sexy lingerie she designed for famous beauties, rock stars, and movie goddesses. Her line had been wildly profitable from the very first year of its existence—of course, charging hundreds of dollars for a few scraps of material had helped. It was all about the image she was able to project, knowing precisely how to do so only too well, as a ex-model herself.

She'd been on countless covers and strutted the catwalk for every designer in Europe until she'd quit at the age of twenty-five and parlayed her saved income into millions. With the help of a wealthy backer, of course—her former lover, who'd noted her business acumen and obtained the necessary financing.

She'd done so well in the previous quarter she would be able to donate her profits to charity after every last supplier and everyone on her staff was paid.

At the founding of her company, she'd vowed to do exactly that someday to honor her mother, an embroiderer and beader, one of the *petite mains,* the little hands, who did the fine sewing and finishing for the great couture houses, behind the scenes in workshops on quiet Parisian streets.

Odette Gaillard now employed several hundred people at her atelier and her showroom. Models flew in from all over the world to work in her dazzling shows, and the most successful men in the world vied for front row seats to watch them.

She smiled inwardly. Most models were too self-obsessed to pay attention to their status-seeking admirers—at least until they left the business, deciding they had a right to eat more than a few hundred grams of food a day.

After she'd quit modeling, Odette had indulged herself for weeks, eating napoleons two at a time and slices of cake to her heart's content, then quit that too, sick of sweets and happy to be done with both extremes. She didn't envy the models and didn't find the business of fashion all that glamorous anymore. But she worked hard.

Surely she was entitled to take a few moments for mental dalliance now and then. Who could he be? She could not remember ever seeing a man so naturally good-looking at one of her shows. Or anywhere else.

Odette watched as he rose to give his seat to Marie Arelquin's grandmother, an ancient but still chic relic of the glory days of French fashion. In the early 1960s, Madame Arelquin had been the most exclusive couturier in Paris, limiting her clients to a handful per year. Odette had read up on the period in her mother's books on fashion, and of course, had pored over Marie's family scrapbooks.

Madame Arelquin had been slim and straight as a reed then, with a matchless style that was all her own. She'd favored pencil-slim skirts topped with flyaway jackets cut very full in the sleeve, immense hats designed to cast an air of mystery, over-the-elbow gloves, and clutch purses.

The Arelquin house had presided over the last era of elegance. After that, it was Courrèges and then Carnaby Street mod and then hippies, until Yves St. Laurent took the look and invented the rich gypsy.

Madame Arelquin had chosen not to fade away, developing a line of facial rejuvenation creams that seemed to work, even though she'd announced in the notoriously catty fashion press that every woman had to choose between her face and her behind at some point. Madame had let the latter get big and round, so that the former would not look starved and sick.

The strategy had worked, Odette noticed. Madame Arelquin had to be over eighty, but she had very few lines on her face. She gave her granddaughter a double air-kiss, not wanting to disturb Marie's *maquillage* or her own carefully applied red lipstick. Odette smiled.

The young man managed a half-bow that was charming and not gauche in the least as he gave up his seat to the *grande dame*. So he had manners. That was a nice plus.

Odette found herself wondering who had taught him to be so respectful of women, and decided that his mother must have instructed him. Whoever she was, she had raised her son right.

Madame Arelquin gave him an imperious nod in return and seated herself next to Marie, crossing her legs elegantly at the ankle as she did.

Odette's other assistant bustled up and looked over her boss's shoulder at the restless crowd through the small opening in the curtain.

"See and be seen. It is always the same," Lucie murmured.

"Ah, there is the winner of the raffle." She pointed the pink eraser end of her pencil at the man now standing behind the Arelquin women, then flipped through her seating chart and made a note on the front row using her own hieroglyphic.

Odette could not read it but it didn't matter. Lucie was a wizard of organization and good at seating the rich and the famous, who slept with each other somewhat indiscriminately. No one who had recently broken up could be put next to an ex, or there was sure to be a cat fight. Amusing, but not good for business.

"I was wondering who he was," Odette said.

"His name is Bryan Bachman. The story is that he spent his last euro on a raffle ticket for your charity and won that seat," Lucie replied.

"Is it true?"

"The reporter says it is." Lucie gave a very French shrug that communicated her doubt. "I am sure he has an ATM card somewhere in those jeans. It is all one needs these days."

"What interest does he have in fashion? Does he want to be a model?"

Lucie shook her head. "I overheard the reporter from *Bonjour Paris* interviewing him in the lobby before the show. Apparently not. He has a degree in science from a California university and is known in his field. Her poor little slave of an assistant went wi-fi and confirmed everything he said on her laptop—I looked over her shoulder while she was doing it. The article will be online in a few hours if you want to look at it."

Odette nodded. She didn't want to wait to read it. "Is he in Paris by himself?"

"I think that is what he said—"

"Where is he staying?" Odette asked, not caring how shamelessly interested she sounded.

"He didn't say, she didn't ask, but I don't think he will sleep on the streets," Lucie said dryly. "Not with that face and that body. He could have his pick of the women here, don't you think?"

"You ask too many rhetorical questions, Lucie. Let's stick to the facts," Odette said.

"I have told you what I know. I thought he looked like a cyclist or a climber, traveling through Europe before he returns to college." Lucie paused to look at him again. "So I was surprised when he said he had a degree. He seems too old to be a student. But he is certainly an athlete."

"I thought the same thing. And Marc did too."

Lucie permitted herself a polite chuckle. "Marc can read the meaning of people's clothes like a detective."

Odette smiled. "Of course. He is a devotee of Hercule Poirot."

"Who is that?" Lucie turned her head in response to a softly voiced call for her assistance. "*Zut.* I am needed. Excuse me."

"Of course," Odette murmured. Every seat was now full, and more people had squeezed in along the walls in back.

Her bouncers were examining invitations and steering a few people who proffered faked ones to the exits. Other assistants scrambled to find folding chairs but inevitably some onlookers would remain standing.

The crowding added to the excitement. So it went. This was her fifth show in as many years. Each one had been more popular than the last.

Odette sighed inwardly as the house lights went down. The walls reflected a deep blue that suggested an undersea realm. She felt at the moment as if she were looking into an aquarium filled with colorful fish, very chic fish with rolling eyes and mouths that opened and closed as they moved about, sometimes in unison and sometimes wriggling frantically when they found themselves alone.

Bryan Bachman seemed out of place among them, but not at a loss. He was self-assured and confident, studying everything he saw with interest. A scientist, hmm? She would not have taken him for one, but she supposed California intellectuals dressed differently.

The Arelquins were doing their best to make conversation with him. Marie Arelquin seemed to be explaining something. Bryan nodded as if he understood and looked up suddenly at the curtain.

At Odette.

She had fancied herself invisible. Apparently not. Odette took a step back. He had to have seen her, so penetrating was his look. Standing there staring, now that the house lights had gone down, she must be visible behind the curtain.

Not that it mattered. Would he even know who she was?

Most likely not. Of course, Lucie saw to it that the creative head of the firm got plenty of publicity, and Odette was photographed often. Still, Bryan Bachman didn't look like someone who read *Vogue* or *Details* or *W*.

The models were lining up not far away behind the curtain, nervous and clumsy in their high heels. They had very little in the way of material to conceal any stumbles or awkward turns on the catwalk, adorned only in the scantiest bras and panties ever seen, and fanciful feather trains and headdresses, which Marc and his team had provided, that harked back to the showgirls of the *Folies Bergère*.

Ready or not, they had to step out. Two or three girls glanced her way, and Odette gave them an encouraging smile.

She let the gap in the curtain fall closed, and went to confer with her makeup people, attending to last-second details, feeling rather distracted.

As soon as the parade down the catwalk was underway, she

could escape and watch most of the show from a distance, as she usually did. It was difficult to get a real feeling of the honest reaction to the new looks otherwise.

Then she would run backstage and emerge at the very end to take a bow.

Who was she?

Bryan had noticed someone behind the curtain from the moment he'd sat down, peeking through. When the house lights went down, he'd seen her in outline.

Fantastic shape, definitely female.

Just before the models stepped out, she'd moved away from there. But he remembered her eyes, intent and watchful as a cat's, outlined with dark pencil. That was about all he could see, but he had a feeling those eyes belonged to someone beautiful.

Then again, everyone at a fashion show this exclusive was beautiful or acted like they were. But the two women on either side of him didn't seem to notice that they were being watched.

The scene was a freakin' zoo otherwise.

And he no longer had a place in the front row, not that he cared. He hadn't expected to win the seat when he'd bought the raffle ticket, just wanted to use up the last of his euros before he flew back home.

He'd come to Paris purely for the hell of it, on his way back from hiking in the Alsace-Lorraine region, on the recommendation of a former roommate. Spectacular scenery, but too damn cold and slippery this time of year.

He somehow imagined that Paris would be warmer. Not in April. He'd stashed his stuff in an inexpensive hotel near the airport, taken the Métro into the heart of the city and wandered around. Brrr.

Bryan understood enough French to know that the French

knew he was American, and left him alone. *Tant pis*, as they said. Tough luck.

The city was interesting, but he didn't have enough money to enjoy much of it, outside of watching the Eiffel Tower light up at night, which was free and very cool.

Even romantic, if he'd had anyone to share it with.

And he'd thought the pretty girl selling raffle tickets was interested in him. Hah.

He'd handed over a couple of bills and jotted down his cell phone number when she'd said something about a charity and a fashion show in the same breath. Whatever.

The text message that he was a winner had surprised him, but he'd had nothing else to do that night. So here he was, making out okay in French, mostly because a lot of them spoke decent English.

Marie Arelquin looked at his tank top and smiled.

"Is that where you are from?" she asked.

He looked down, not remembering what he had on right away. "Uh—yeah. Newport Beach. I grew up there but I've lived all over California."

Two really young women in the next row leaned over to take a look too. See and be seen, he thought. He was hardly God's gift to fashion, but they eyed him appreciatively.

The first nodded wisely. "*Le O.C.*," she said to her friend as if he wasn't able to figure out what that meant.

"*Non. Baywatch*," her friend replied.

"They think you are an actor," Marie whispered.

He looked back at the girls to see if they'd heard her say that, but they were busy gawking at some other guy, who actually was famous.

Bryan couldn't blame them for the mistake, since he was dressed like a lifeguard on the lam. Couldn't be helped. He'd dug out the wetsuit jacket because the weather was cold, and it offered lightweight warmth. The tank top had been underneath it in his duffel bag. He hadn't put on his sweater, underestimating how damp it was.

Everything else he owned was dirty, including his underwear, but he wasn't staying in the kind of hotel that had laundry service. So, he'd shown up in take-me-as-I-am mode.

Milling around before the show started was interesting and the people-watching was a hoot. So this was what fashionistas were like. He'd memorized every detail he could to share with his mother in his next e-mail, and then made friends with Marie Arelquin, a sophisticate who didn't seem to mind his funky clothes or his shaggy hair, and who didn't try to hit on him, either.

Talking to Marie was fun and her English was a lot better than his French. And what could he do but give up his seat to her grandmother when she'd edged through the crowd?

Madame Arelquin was or had been a big deal in this weird world, judging by the deferential nods she got, but these days she apparently wasn't quite as big a deal as Mademoiselle Arelquin, right up front. He was getting an idea of the hierarchy involved, and feeling a little like he'd gone back in time to the court of the Sun King. Bow and scrape. Check out each other's clothes and shoes.

As far as that went, the old lady had eyed him haughtily from head to toe, and Bryan got the message. His own mother would have been proud of how fast he'd been to offer the coveted front-row chair to her.

The music thundered and the show began.

Bryan stood behind the Arelquins, who were talking in rapid-fire French that he half-understood as one leggy babe after another strode by at the level of his nose. The first two or three made his cock twitch—high heels and underwear were an effective combination—but after a while, the models and what they were wearing began to blur in his mind.

Something about the way they walked was off-putting. Their bodies were unnatural, for one thing. Their legs were extremely thin, and so were their arms. And their butts were just too flat. Boobs, non-existent. Were there guys who got off on women this skinny and underfed?

Bryan liked the kind of female you could get a grip on. These girls looked breakable.

Never mind, he told himself. Just get the details. He knew his mother wouldn't believe he'd gotten a front-row seat at a designer show. But that reporter from *Bonjour Paris* had had him pose for pictures before they entered the showroom hall, and made the photographer guy promised to e-mail Bryan the jpegs that same night.

The photographer, who was the essence of arty cool in a shaved head, Harley tattoo, T-shirt, and a black leather vest, never looked at Bryan except through the image finder. But he'd said yes. Bryan figured he'd stop at an internet café and forward whatever popped up in his e-mail as soon as he could.

Come to think of it, he'd post them on Facebook. His UC Santa Cruz postgrad pals would be sure to get on his case about the political incorrectness of a fashion show.

He'd get a more honest reaction from his minimum-wage-earning, wave-riding, jock friends. They'd either laugh their skanky heads off or die of envy. And then there was the head of the marine biology department, a lonesome weirdo they all called the Giant Squid. The Squid would want to get his tentacles on a model, no doubt about it.

"Bryan," Marie was saying. "Do you want to go out after the show to eat with me and my grandmother?"

He loved the way she said that. *Grrranmuzzaire.* It sounded better than just plain grandmother and her lips looked so pretty as she parted them, waiting for his reply. But even so. Hitting on a woman with her formidable grandmother right by her side? Nope. Wasn't going to happen.

"Ah—no. Sorry. I have a, uh, previous engagement." That sounded lame, he thought.

It would have to do. He didn't have enough money to take her and Madame Arelquin out, and he wasn't going to let them take him out.

Marie only smiled and nodded, and returned her attention to the show, making notes on a pad of paper. Laptops weren't allowed, she'd said. She'd explained that new designs were often copied within hours of their appearance on catwalks. So, no cellphones, no cameras.

He edged his way into an opening between her chair and the next, and squatted down on his haunches. A passing model looked down with surprise and gave him a startled smile. The occupant of the chair to Marie's right, a tycoon type in an impeccably tailored suit, glared at him.

Bryan grinned back. The model, seventeen at most, hadn't even noticed the tycoon, who was undoubtedly a model hound. The dude had to be in his fifties, though. But obviously rich. Happy hunting, Bryan thought with disgust.

"I appreciate the invitation, Marie. You've been great about explaining all this." He gestured toward the stage as he turned his attention again to Marie. "Thanks."

"Is crazy, no?"

"Yes. But fun in a way."

"For me, it is work."

Her grandmother, on Marie's left, leaned over and got his attention with a crooked finger. "So you are enjoying the show?"

"Sure." Bryan glanced up at an improbably high pair of cork-soled wedge sandals clomping by. The model dragged an equally improbable swath of peacock feathers after her, raising a faint swirl of dust.

"The girls are beautiful," Madame Arelquin said with approval.

"*Oui,*" Bryan said. It seemed like the only thing he could say. And he wasn't totally lying. They were amazing in their gangly, gorgeous way, just not his type.

He couldn't imagine actually dating one. He would feel guilty sinking his teeth into a juicy BLT while they, what, sucked on toothpicks and sipped ice water?

Besides, you probably couldn't even get a BLT in Paris. Or a chili dog. Two things he really craved.

He was hungry, and truth be told, he didn't know if he could make it to the end of this fashion extravagoonzah, especially because he didn't know how long it was going to last.

Model after model appeared, in teeny thongs and fancy bras. The effect was oddly unerotic. Plus the noise of the throbbing techno music, and the crush of heavily made-up, perfumed, overdressed women—okay, there were a few men in the mix but so what—it was giving him an headache.

He rose, made some excuse in half-assed French that the very nice Arelquins accepted, and got as far as the back wall.

And there she was. The woman whose eyes he had seen behind the curtain. Killer curves, long legs. The shadow template stuck in his head.

"Hello," he said. He wasn't going to ask why she'd been peeking out. She must have something to do with the show, probably was a production coordinator or something like that. He tried to think of the French for headache, so he could ask her if she had one too, and couldn't remember it to save his life.

Hell, he could do better than that for small talk. He didn't want to sound like a hypochondriac. Bryan hoped she spoke

English. A lot of the Parisians around his age seemed to, and she was obviously only a few years older than he was, if that. Worth a shot.

"Great show," he said. That seemed like a safe opening line.

"Thank you." She looked toward the stage, observing the models stalking down it, executing their turns with thousand-yard stares over the audience, and heading back behind the curtain.

Bryan looked at her. Whoever she was, she had style. French women knew how to dress. The outfit was one of a kind, almost like she'd put together bits and pieces from a thrift shop.

She had on a fitted black jacket with a big lapel pin of a pelican that made him smile. Underneath that was a camisole—was that what those tight tops were called? Maybe it was a corset. Anyway, it was low-cut and made of black lace that stretched over beautiful full breasts.

Get a grip, he told himself, wishing in another second that that particular verb hadn't come to mind. Of course, he did want to get his hands on that sweet flesh. *No, you jerk. Keep your eyes moving.*

Bryan drew in a breath. No matter where he looked, she made him hot. He glanced down at a short skirt in hot pink showing off strong, slender legs that got that way because she undoubtedly walked a lot and bicycled and danced. And jumped for joy.

Something about her said that uninhibited joy was part of the deal.

Yeah.

What would it feel like to have legs like that clasped around his lower back while he—*you don't even know her name.*

She was talking to him. "I heard you won a ticket to a front row seat."

"Huh?" He lifted his gaze from her shoes, which were

strapped at the ankle, high-heeled but cut low, with toe cleavage. She had been tapping one foot idly, which had gotten his attention. He was pretty sure her stockings were seamed. He'd love to bend her over and find out if garters were involved. "Oh—right. Quite a view. I've never been to anything like this."

"I can tell." There was a mischievous gleam in her eyes.

Now he was close enough to see their color—green with dashes of gold. But it was the expression in them that mesmerized him. Soulful. Intelligent. Woman-of-the-world.

Whereas he, Bryan Bachman, was still knocking around said world, waiting to hear from graduate schools while he tried to figure out what he wanted to do with his life. She looked like she had. She looked successful, despite her thrift store outfit, which was cute as hell.

"Hey, would you like to get out of here and get something to eat?" he said all of a sudden. "How about a BLT? My treat."

Big spender. But he could probably afford that. She actually seemed pleased. He would have sworn that she blushed for a second, and was amazed when she did.

"Ah, what is a BLT?" she asked politely.

"That's a bacon, lettuce, and tomato sandwich," he explained. "I've been craving one. It's really simple and really good, when you get the ingredients right. The tomato has to be ripe and the mayonnaise is key—"

"It sounds very American," she said thoughtfully. "But then we French invented mayonnaise."

"Yeah." Bryan stuck his hands in the pockets of his jeans, wondering if he'd made a mistake. He should have asked her out to a good bistro, not that he knew one from another. Of course, he could have asked her to recommend one. And risk sounding like a mooch? No way.

He didn't even know where to get a decent BLT in Paris, let alone whether she'd like his favorite sandwich.

"So you want American food," she was saying. "We can go to Le Diner, then."

"You know a place?"

She nodded. "The chef is as French as I am, but the cuisine is definitely not."

"Is that a good thing or a bad thing?" Bryan asked sheepishly.

Odette had to laugh. "I have heard only good things about it, but I have never been there. I do know that tourists haven't discovered it yet—it just opened."

"Okay, that's a good thing. I won't run into anyone I know from back home."

Odette gave him a look of mock offense. "Why? Are you ashamed to be seen with me?"

"Hell, no," he said, flashing a startled smile. "You must be the hottest woman in Paris. If you don't mind my saying so."

"Not at all." She gave him a smile that melted him.

"Anyway, I'd much rather look at you than a bunch of fanny-packers."

"Ah. I see. *Merci, m'sieu.*"

He looked around at the filled-to-capacity hall as if he had no idea where he was and gave one last absent-minded glance at the catwalk. The music was louder and the models were dancing now, working the crowd.

The model hound in the row he'd left reached up and tried to grab an ankle. Bryan noticed the beefiest bouncer heading that way.

"*Cochon,*" Odette said indignantly. "There is one at every show."

"He is a pig. Do you want me to—"

She shook her head. "The situation is under control."

The tycoon was being lifted off his feet and hauled away faster than he could call a lawyer.

20

"All right. Well . . . shall we go?" He'd gotten lucky, she'd said yes, and he wanted to leave before anything else distracted her.

"Yes."

Bryan looked around, somewhat disoriented by the place and the ever-louder music. They must be getting around to the grand finale.

"Lead the way," he said to her.

She shook her head. "That's not how I like to do things." She stepped forward and slid her arm around his. "You are the man, no?"

"Uh . . . yeah. I like the way you say that."

It took several minutes to get near the exit. He seemed even taller that close. His body so near hers, his thighs brushing hers, made her think of what she wanted: sex. Uncomplicated by emotion. But as passionate as two people who didn't really know each other could make it.

Not just yet. She needed to find out more about him, look him up online, confirm Lucie's offhand remarks. Odette whispered a few words to one of the bouncers on her way out so Marc would not worry.

Looking into the mirror of the bathroom in Le Diner, Odette asked herself a few interesting questions as she reapplied her eye pencil.

The first was *What do you think you are doing?* And the second, which was trickier, was *When are you going to tell him who you are?*

He didn't seem to realize that she was Odette Gaillard of Oh! Oh! Odette Lingerie, hadn't asked her name. Just talked to her, half in schoolboy French that made her giggle, half in English, in between bites of his BLT. Even better, he'd listened when she talked.

But she'd been a little evasive, taking advantage of his not-so-fluent French to avoid questions. She'd ordered a BLT too. He was right. The sandwich was very good and very much the sort of thing one could crave.

So was he. Bryan Bachman was exactly what she wanted right now, and she needed a fling.

On a mad impulse, she'd deliberately skipped the grand finale of her own show. Missed her bow. Done without the loud acclaim of the crowd in attendance and the kissyface insincerity of the well-wishers afterward.

Odette had realized in the moment when Bryan had asked her out that she needed a holiday from the hoopla.

After five shows, she knew only too well that buyers would buy. Sex always sold.

Her designs were flirty and fun, of no real consequence. Her collection escaped the criticism reserved for true haute couture: the deconstructionists of fashion who turned garments inside out, and the architects of fabric whose pleats and poufs made women's bodies invisible.

Marc had probably seized the opportunity to take her bow for her, and accept the bouquets of roses like the beauty pageant winner he longed to be in his retro fantasies of glamour.

Bless Marc's gender-bending heart. Her assistant would be the first to understand a mad impulse to have a bizarre but tasty sandwich with a stranger. And whatever happened next.

Odette straightened her pelican pin, touched up her lipstick, and went out the swinging door, back to Bryan.

He'd finished the sandwich and was tackling a plate of *frites.* He looked up when she slid into the opposite side of the booth.

"This place is great. They didn't miss a trick." He gestured with a *frite* toward the quilted steel walls and the mirrored tile above it that reflected the cakes and pies in a glass-doored cabinet behind the counter.

Odette took another *frite* from his plate and nibbled at the end of it. "I am glad you like it."

He studied her. "I like the way you eat that."

"What do you mean?" She set it down on her plate.

"Like it was forbidden fruit. But you eat it anyway."

"It is." She took a sip of coke. "I am in the fashion business."

"Right. I haven't even asked you what it is you do exactly. Or your name."

"Odette." She waved the napkin she picked up from the table again as if that were enough of an answer to the rest of it.

"Just Odette?"

"Odette Gaillard." She watched his face. Her name didn't seem to register with him one way or another.

"Pretty name," he said. "But then everything sounds pretty in French."

She hesitated, not sure whether to explain more and not wanting to at all. A fling was a fling. Explaining who she was would feel something like handing him a balance sheet or pulling up an e-file of press clippings on her company. For a little while longer, she wanted to be no more than herself.

"So what was it that you do again?" he asked.

"Ah, I am a stylist." That wasn't so very far from the truth.

"That means that you . . . style things?" He gave her a hopeful look.

"Yes."

"Help me out here. I'm just a guy. What does that mean?"

Odette picked up another *frite* and ate it in two bites. Fried food gave her courage. "If I were to style an outfit for an American athlete, I would go to the flea markets and vintage clothing stores to buy exactly what you have on. A tank top from a famous beach and a wetsuit jacket—"

"Actually, neoprene is too hot to walk around in where I'm from, but Paris is cold in the spring, so it works. At home I wouldn't be wearing it except when I'm actually in the water."

She glanced at the faded letters on his tank top. "Newport Beach? I have seen it on that TV show. The harbor is huge."

Bryan nodded. "Yeah. And filled with luxury yachts that the owners never sail. They make pretty good roosts for the pelicans." He nodded at the pin on her lapel. "I like that. Made me think of them."

"Ah. What else is there in Newport Beach besides pelicans?"

"Beach shacks that sell for two million dollars. Hamburgers that cost twenty dollars. The real people got priced out a while ago. But there are a few crazy kayakers left."

"Not surfers?"

"Farther south you get surfers. Newport Beach doesn't have big waves, as a rule."

"Oh. I imagined you as a surfer."

Bryan laughed a little ruefully. "Okay, you're not wrong. But I had to hit Highway 1 to get anywhere worth surfing."

"I have heard of it. In *Le O.C.*"

He made a wry face. "Not my favorite show."

Odette nodded. "It is for teenagers, *non?*"

"That's about right."

She let her gaze move over his well-muscled body. Bryan was very much a man. "So what is it that you do?" she asked him at last.

"Short version?"

"If you please."

"I'm twenty-five. No brothers or sisters. Raised by my mom. She's a dressmaker—I can't wait to send her the photos from before the show. She won't believe I got to see Paris fashion on the runway."

Odette raised an eyebrow. So the interviewer from *Bonjour*

hadn't been able to resist having photos taken of Bryan because of his raffle win. Not much of a story, that, but Bryan himself was delectable. No doubt the witch, as Lucie called her, had been all over him like a—like a wetsuit. And not just the jacket.

"Got a BA in marine biology from the University of California at Santa Cruz, halfway through my master's," Bryan was saying. "I took time off to travel. Went up the Amazon for a while and did independent study in Belize. Right now the Scripps Institute has me waiting to hear." He smiled at her puzzled look. "It's in San Diego. The best marine lab in the US, outside of Woods Hole in Massachusetts. I applied there too. In fact, I applied to every university within swimming distance of a barnacle."

"I see. So what brought you to Paris?"

"Last stop before my flight home." He looked at her a little worriedly. "Not that I didn't want to see Paris. But I'm not that much of a city guy."

"How much of the city have you seen?"

He pushed the plate of *frites* away. "I'm ashamed to say it. Not much. The Eiffel Tower. The cheap tour of the Champs-Élysées. The back end of Notre Dame, from a tour boat on the Seine. And the depressing lobby of my budget hotel."

"And how much time do you have left?" Odette asked.

"Two more nights. Which is to say that I have to check out by Friday. After that I don't really have to be anywhere."

"Then you can stay with me if you like."

"What?"

Odette, per the unwritten rules of flings, didn't explain her invitation.

"For starters," she said airily. "Do you like jazz?"

"Sure. Anything but techno. No offense, Odette, because you work for whoever runs that fashion show, but the music was the pits."

"Then we will go to the Bistrot d'Eustache or the China Club. They have wicked gin fizzes."

"Sign me up. And lead the way." She began to protest but he held up a hand. "You have to. I'm a stranger in a strange land, Odette."

"How melodramatic," she said with disdain.

"I can see I'm going to have to prove I'm the man."

Odette felt a secret flush of excitement steal through her. His tone of voice was teasing, but there was an underlying edge in it that made it clear he understood what she wanted from him. No-strings-attached sensuality. Fast and furious. Clandestine—she had no particular wish to tell him who she was. No, she wanted an affair with no limits except time. Necessarily brief.

But intense.

Later . . .

It was well after midnight when they left the China Club. Odette had gambled on seeing no one she knew there, and she'd been right. Marc and Lucie and the rest of her staff had gone off to a boîte in the Rue du Faubourg St.-Denis to celebrate—she'd received a text message from Marc that was a perfect combination of tact and innuendo as to the reason for her disappearance. The models had gone back to their hotels to collapse.

Giddy from one too many gin fizzes, they had hailed a taxi and come back to her apartment in the most exclusive *arrondissement* in Paris.

She hoped he wouldn't realize that.

The elegant buildings stood in regular rows, their mansard roofs neatly aligned, their stone blocks punctuated by wrought-iron balconies. It was too early in spring and too cold for flow-

26

ers to spill from them—and even with the old-fashioned street-lights, rather too dark to see much.

He made no comment. Perhaps he thought the neighborhood was old-fashioned. She was counting on his lack of knowledge of Paris—after not wanting him to know she was famous, she really didn't want him to know that she was rich.

It would change the mood of this brief affair, from the happiness of a man and a woman without a thought for anything but their delight in each other and their mutual desire for each other to something very different.

She unlocked the outer door of wrought iron and the inner one, then led him up the curving marble staircase to the third floor.

"Oh my. Watching you go up the stairs is serious motivation." A few steps behind her, he reached up to stroke the inside of her thigh. Odette paused, thrilled by the sensual tickle of a male hand on her silk stockings.

But Bryan didn't reach all the way up. Or grab. He sighed and let his hand trail down, then patted her calf. "Keep going or we'll never get there."

Odette giggled and continued to mount the stairs, knowing that her short skirt was swishing provocatively only inches from his face.

She wouldn't mind if he lifted it and pressed kisses on her bottom, which was mostly bare. He didn't know that because he hadn't touched it.

A young man who wanted to wait, was able to wait, could savor every moment of the foreplay—sex with Bryan Bachman ought to be good. Very good.

She opened the door to her apartment and motioned him in, switching on a light.

"Wow. Nice place." He looked around at the furnishings. "You have interesting stuff." He ran a hand over an armchair made of slabs of clear lucite that had red roses embedded in it, stems and all. "Is this for sitting in or is this a work of art?"

"You can sit in it if you like."

"That didn't answer my question." He turned around and settled himself in it. "Not very comfortable. I prefer upholstery."

Odette pointed to a sofa thickly padded in dark green velvet. "Then sit there."

"Only if you do." He looked at the naked nymphs carved on the legs of the low table in front of the sofa before he stretched out. "Now that's something you generally don't see on an American coffee table."

"Why not?"

"No bare breasts allowed on the furniture, I guess. They seem to be everywhere in Paris. Even on the billboards."

Odette held her breath. The taxi had passed a huge ad for her company screened onto vinyl and attached to the side of a building. Had he noticed the Oh! Oh! Odette logo?

Apparently not.

"I just have to get used to it," Bryan was saying. "I bet you don't give bare boobs a second thought, not with a job like yours."

"Not really, no."

He gave the table an admiring look. "So where'd you get this thing?"

"Les Puces. The flea market. It's a Victorian piece. Not valuable. I just liked it."

"Okay." He leaned back against the cushions and looked around at the rest of the room. "Works with everything else. I like your style, Odette. I like everything about you. Come here."

For some reason, the exuberant compliment and the command that followed it made her nervous.

"In a moment." She sauntered into the kitchen, feeling very

hungry and needing something to eat that would soak up the drinks they'd downed.

There was bread, plain bread, but it was exactly what she wanted. Odette extracted the long, uncut baguette from its crackling paper bag and went back into the living room with it, along with a corked, half-full bottle of wine and two glasses held dexterously in her fingers. He'd moved to the couch.

"You look like an ad for Air France," he chuckled.

"Do I? The bread is very good. Still fresh." She extended the long loaf to him. "Feel it."

He gave it a squeeze and looked at her, laughing. "Is this some kind of crazy French sex ritual?" he asked, after she plopped down next to him. He accepted the morsel of bread she tore off and put into his mouth, and didn't talk for a little while.

"Yes," she said. Odette had several bites and so did he before he took the baguette away and set it on the coffee table.

"Mmm. A loaf of bread, a jug of wine, and thou. And a naked table. It doesn't get better."

She planted a kiss lightly dusted with flour on his cheek. "You must be part French."

He nuzzled her neck. "Don't think so."

"What are you then?" she asked. What he was doing felt very good.

"A red-blooded, all-American man," he growled. "That okay with you?"

"*Bien sûr,*" she murmured.

His lips pressed against the side of her neck for several sensual kisses before he opened his mouth and nipped her. The contact was immediately erotic, almost dominating.

Odette arched her back and let him do it, wanting only to melt into his arms and let him take over.

2

———————

Bryan's hand rested easily on her thigh and the sensation warmed her flesh all the way up to her pussy.

Odette wriggled, settling more deeply between his spread thighs. His old jeans were soft against the sheer silk of her stockings, and she found herself wanting to rub her bottom upon those strong thighs while he still wore them.

Of course, he still didn't know that only narrow garters covered that part of her. The scrap of silk that served to cover her labia—barely—was held on by the thinnest possible straps that curved over her hips and slid into the crease of skin where her thighs ended.

The thong ended there.

Bryan gave a sexually charged sigh as her ass, still confined by the short, hot pink skirt, pressed against his fly.

She could feel his erection. Ahhh. Long. Getting longer. She wanted to rip the already torn jeans open and see exactly what he had. But she had a feeling they were the only pair he had. Besides, they were probably irreplaceable. With him inside them, they were irresistible.

Odette wriggled out of her jacket and flung it aside. She still had on her black lace cami top, what there was of it. Her breasts were nearly overflowing it, thanks to the black lace bra underneath, which took the concept of push-up to a new high. She stroked his face, then began to kiss him the way she liked to kiss: deep and slow. And then she began to rub herself in his lap.

Bryan gave a soft groan that she captured, sucking it away along with his breath.

Poor man. He was having a hard time letting her pleasure and stimulate herself. She broke off the kiss and let her hands drift down, feeling his biceps under the neoprene jacket.

His hands were still holding her, but the muscles in his arms bulged, then released, then bulged again from the sexual tension that her pleasurable *frottage* was causing.

She whimpered sensually into his ears. "I like to rub this way. May I?"

"Jesus." He gritted his teeth as the sacrilegious epithet escaped. "Do whatever you want. Just don't stop."

Disobeying just to see what he would do, Odette rose slightly, bracing her hands on his broad shoulders, but she wasn't quick enough. Bryan grabbed her hips and pushed her back down, hard, groaning as the soft, feminine flesh of her bottom hit his hard cock.

And he still hadn't seen it, still didn't know her ass was, for all intents and purposes, naked and available.

Wantonly, Odette pulled up the hem and showed him what he'd been missing. First the front of the thong. And then she took one of his hands and moved it behind her.

He touched the bare, heated flesh with a look of mingled lust and wonder. "You mean you weren't wearing anything but this?"

"No. I wanted you to reach up and find that out for yourself."

"Oh, Odette." He made up for lost time, using both hands to fondle her behind.

"I like to be stroked while I rub a man's thighs," she whispered into his ear.

"God. Do it then."

Odette rose again but this time he didn't stop her, just kept his hands where they were while she stepped into a straddle that encompassed both his legs. She used hers to push his thighs together, despite their heavy muscle. Holding the hot pink skirt up to her waist.

His eyes widened and he seemed to be looking at something behind her. Odette smiled before she sat back down in his lap. The mirror on the opposite wall gave him a good view of that XXX-rated pose: seamed stockings, their wide tops pulled into points by the thin garters hooked into them.

Skirt up. Bottom bared. His hands on it.

Yes. She knew he saw exactly that because she felt his hands begin to spread her buttocks.

"Bend over," he said hoarsely. "Like you're going to tease me with your beautiful big breasts."

This time she obeyed. But she waited to hear what he was going to say next. He was still looking over her shoulder at the back view of her in the mirror.

Then he suddenly spread her ass cheeks completely apart, not gently, and she gave a little cry. He held her that way. She strained a little, tightening anally as her labia parted with a juicy noise. Odette began to pant. His unexpected but controlled moment of roughness excited her.

"Now I see pink," he growled. "Your pussy is swollen. All that rubbing does you good."

"Yes."

"Put your fingers in yourself, mademoiselle."

She rested her head on his shoulder and gave him a hot little show. One finger slid in, then two. He kept her behind fully spread and didn't say a thing.

"Do you like to watch women masturbate?" she murmured.

"Uh-huh. Your little anus tightens when you fingerfuck yourself. Did you know that?"

"No," Odette said.

"Maybe it's because I'm spreading you nice and wide. I can really see everything."

Now he was getting down and dirty. She loved it.

He gave her ass a final squeeze, then pulled her down into his lap.

"Don't you want to get undressed?" she asked.

"Soon. Not yet. If you like to rub your hot pussy on denim, then I want to see more of that. I like getting you undressed little by little."

Odette straddled him again. He slid a finger under the patch of sheer silk at the front of her thong.

"Shaved but not all the way," he muttered. "Good. I like some curls to play with too." He twined the exploring finger into a few and gave a light tug.

Her clitoris was revealed by the move and she strained forward. "Touch me, Bryan."

He kept the skin lifted by his light pull on her intimate curls, and did as she asked, touching a finger of his other hand to the very tip of her clit.

"Slick," he said.

He applied infinitesimal pressure to her clit tip, pulling a little harder on her pubic curls to keep that sensitive bit of flesh forward and up so he could fool around with it.

34

But there was nothing foolish about what he was doing. If there was a term like sexual intelligence, that would apply.

He massaged her clit, just her clit, on the sides, then moved the hood of it back, beginning a stimulation that was so sensual it was almost uncomfortable.

Odette could imagine what he could do with his mouth if his fingers were this skillful. Oh God. That was going to happen.

She let him play with her tiny rod, looking down. His chest rose and fell with the deep breaths he took. Bryan was intent upon what he was doing, exploring every nuance of her sexual response.

Underneath his moving fingers was the huge bulge of his cock and balls, pressed back by his old jeans.

If anything could burst the well-worn denim, it would be a cock that size, she thought. The long rod was on one side of the fly, where the material had worn so thin that the head was clearly outlined atop the shaft.

She reached through his hands to run a finger down the hot curve of flesh. Restrained, his erection was forced against his upper thigh. She reached farther down.

His heavy balls strained against the frazzled seam at the center of his jeans, so big that he had to keep his legs separated far apart.

Her fingertips rubbed him there provocatively and Bryan moaned. Then he gritted his teeth and shifted on the sofa, taking his fingers away from her clit and bringing them to his nose.

"That is the most delicate scent of a woman ever," he murmured. "Clean but extremely sexual. Your clit is giving it up."

"Can it do that?"

"Seems so." He put his finger back on the tip of her clit, and rubbed it until it tingled.

She leaned forward and whispered into his ear. "I used to wonder what it felt like to ejaculate. I always wanted to."

"It's a rush," Bryan said. "A pulsing, hot rush. Can't control it."

"I want to come in your hand."

"No coming."

She pouted and he smiled.

"Let me amend that. Not yet."

Odette didn't want him to take his finger away but he did.

"These haven't gotten any attention," he mused, moving his hands to her breasts. He reached inside her cami top and felt one, then brought it out of her bra. Then the other.

Odette shivered. The difference between the cooler air of the room and the heat of the silken material that had cupped and uplifted her was noticeable. Her nipples stood out, long and pink.

She used her palms to warm and stroke her breasts, then made light circles over her nipples. "Ahhh," she moaned. "Suck. They need to be sucked."

"I love a bossy chick," he said softly, "I don't have to wonder about what you want. You tell me, I do it." He immediately applied his mouth to a nipple and suckled her tenderly.

"I like to be bossed too," she murmured. The inside of her pussy tensed with each pull of his strong lips and tongue.

He stopped for a second. "We'll get around to that. Give and take."

Her other nipple was happy with the lascivious attention it got next. Odette twined her hands in his thick, tousled hair, and worked with him to intensify her own pleasure, pulling back so that her nipple was drawn out, forcing him to suck hard to keep it.

She loved men like this, at the breast, squeezing and sucking and reveling in female flesh. She suspected that most were indulging fantasies from boyhood on, when they'd sneaked looks at every woman with a pretty bosom, longing to touch it freely and be held against it.

Bryan was no different from other men in that regard. His hand clasped one, his lips sought the nipple of the other, and he loved it with his mouth almost worshipfully.

Odette shifted on his spread thighs. Her thong did nothing to absorb the sensual slickness that made her intimate flesh smell so sweet to him. But she was so excited that her labia had swelled together, trapping the juice of excitement inside.

One rub from his hand and his palm would be wet. She wanted him to do it.

Odette straightened up, gently pushing his head back. Her nipple popped out of his mouth, which he wiped roughly with the back of his hand, his eyes on the tender tip.

He reached up to tug on the other, exciting it to the same length as the just-sucked one. "Gotta even them out," he said with a grin.

"Mmm." Odette took his hand and moved it to between her legs. "Rub my pussy," she commanded, "the whole thing. Rub and squeeze."

Lazily, he did just that, watching her eyes drift half-closed.

Just as she'd thought. The intimate caress made her swollen labia part and his hand became as slick as she was.

"You're so wet," he murmured. "I feel like you came in my hand."

"I didn't."

"Good girl. I want to get you a lot more excited than this."

She reached down and took his hand by the wrist, bringing it to her lips and darting her tongue into the center of his palm.

"Look at you licking yourself up," he growled. "Dainty as a kitten."

Odette cleaned his palm without replying, then took his fingers into her mouth, sucking each one just as clean.

"Like the way you taste?"

"Mm-hm," she murmured, sucking and licking.

He let her finish, then let her cup his damp hand to her flushed cheek.

"Interesting," he said. "Very interesting. What else do you like in your mouth?"

Odette answered by resting her hand on the front of his jeans. "It's time, *n'est-ce pas?*"

"Yeah." He gazed into her eyes so long and so deeply that she was a little disconcerted. Then he moved her off his lap, half-lifting her with ease.

He stood as she sprawled sensually on the sofa, her legs far apart, watching him shuck the flexible jacket and the tank top in one go. His chest was perfect, carved out of ripped muscle and sleek skin with just a dusting of dark hair over his pecs.

Her eyes followed the line it made down his hard abs, dividing them and diving under his jeans.

No belt. He flicked the round steel button at the waistband out of its tattered buttonhole and fumbled for the zipper, distracted by the way she was staring at his crotch.

"Let me," Odette whispered. She kneeled on the sofa and found the tiny shank of steel that opened the zipper, caressing his imprisoned cock as she pulled the zipper slowly open.

Her hands moved the two sides of the front of his jeans apart, and she pressed kisses to the soft cotton of the briefs beneath that still concealed his hard, hot rod.

From the root to the head, it was too long and too thick to spring out. Bryan groaned and eased a hand into her hair, pushing her head against his trapped flesh.

Odette pressed kiss after kiss to the shaft, then nipped it through the cotton knit. He stiffened, then trembled. She loved him like this, not knowing what he was going to get, up for anything.

He put a finger under her chin and lifted her head, looking

into her eyes again. His were blazing with desire. He pushed her back a little on the sofa, then worked his jeans down over his hips. The briefs came with them.

And there it was.

The biggest, thickest cock she'd ever seen, jutting out of dark curls at its base, moving in a way he couldn't really control. Toward her.

Odette's lips parted at the sight.

Bryan Bachman, his jeans halfway down his beautifully muscled thighs, would stumble if he took one step. Which he meant he was rooted to the spot.

He grabbed at the top of his jeans, eager to finish the struggle of getting out of them, but her stilling hand intervened.

"Stop," she said. "Just as you like me half-undressed, I like you the same way. Jeans pulled down like that are very provocative. A male ass suddenly revealed is beautiful."

"You haven't seen that," he said, keeping his hands where they were.

"Turn around," was her reply. "Show off."

"Okay, this is gay. But whatever."

"No, it isn't," she whispered when he indulged her whim. Odette reached out to caress his fine, hard, bare ass. It was completely smooth and tanned all over.

He relaxed, beginning to enjoy himself. "Yeah, I swim naked," he said in response to a question she hadn't thought to ask. Then she remembered that Americans generally didn't. "I like to be in wild places, remember? No one around to be shocked."

"Ah, what a pleasure it would be to see you naked in the woods," she murmured. She ran her hands over the hollows at the sides of his buttocks. He trembled like a horse, his hard haunches apart despite the jeans that bunched around them. "Push them lower," she instructed, wanting him to reveal himself.

"Not tired of the view? I can go panoramic," he said. He twisted and looked at her over his shoulder. That deep-carved dimple flashed in his cheek.

Which would bring that magnificent cock directly opposite her lips at some point. The temptation to suck it would be too strong to resist. No, she would play with him this way for a little while.

"In a moment," she replied, catching his amused gaze. "Bend over first. Just as you are."

He snorted but he didn't turn around. "Now that really is gay."

"It is sexy to see a man from behind," she insisted. "The balls on display, the cock out in front—the gay men know a few things."

"No surprises," he muttered as he bent, bracing his hands on his knees. He adjusted the pushed-down denims, which were tangled with his briefs.

"Look but don't touch?" she asked.

"You can touch. Just leave the hole alone. I can play with yours. You can't play with mine."

"Silly. I had no intention of it." Still, she looked. It was tight and small and clean. His willingness to take such a vulnerable pose pleased her. Odette insinuated her hand between his thighs, stroking the sensitive flesh at the insides and top. He sighed with pleasure. She could see his balls tighten.

They were next.

She cupped them and his whole body tensed. How heavy they were in her hand, hot from their confinement in his jeans.

Her wriggling in his lap had excited him deeply. He would come hard for her, shooting jets of come upon her willing flesh if she asked for it, she was sure of it.

Odette reached further, stroking his cock from the root to just under the tip. There had to be a drop of pre-come trembling on the head, hot and thick. Too thick to fall until he turned around and she could lick it up as daintily as she'd licked her juice from his palm.

Bryan gave a growl as he stood up and turned around. "Enough. The rest of me is getting lonely."

Odette rested her hands over his as he pushed the jeans down to his knees. She sat back as he stepped out of them.

"Naked at last. But you stay the way you are. The lingerie is great. Is that from the company you work for?"

"No." She didn't always wear her own designs, fortunately for her tonight. He wouldn't be finding an Oh! Oh! Odette label when he took it all off.

"Whatever. I don't care. I love black lace." His hands on his hips, his cock proud and out, he looked down at it. "Yeah. A lot."

"Good. I can see that." And she saw the drop of come she'd anticipated. Odette reached out a finger and took it off, showing him the glistening moisture on her fingertip before she popped it into her mouth, savoring it. "You are delicious."

He took a couple of steps closer. "Lie back. Lift your legs. Show off your pussy. I didn't really get a chance to see it."

Odette reclined lazily, lifting her legs and spreading them as wide as she could. The thong was on crooked, but that would give him a better view fo the feminine flesh he'd treated so tenderly.

He kneeled in front of her and pushed it farther to the side. It drifted back. He took the straps and snapped them, then tossed it aside.

"Bit by bit," he murmured. His head came down as his mouth took her clit. He sucked like a master, pulsing his lips in time with her pulse. The erotic sensation was incredible.

He moved down in a few minutes, telling her again that he didn't want her to come yet.

Noelle Mack

Odette moaned her acquiescence. On her back, she didn't feel like giving orders. She was more than ready to have him take charge. Except that . . . she would enjoy oral even more if her own mouth were filled, if his strong thighs trapped her head while he pressed his balls to her mouth.

She could take at least one at a time, lapping it with her tongue, then the other. If he would let her control the downward thrust of his cock by encircling it with her fingers, she could take that too.

"Please," she begged, *"soixante-neuf."*

"Sixty-nine?"

"Oui. Come over me. I want to suck cock."

He didn't argue, they assumed the position, and Odette felt waves of very powerful arousal begin deep inside her.

Penetrated by his strong tongue, she returned the favor by sucking hard on his cock, taking as much of it as she could. Her encircling fingers were slick from her mouth, giving him a channel to slide in and out of that was so wet and tight, he moaned.

She didn't care what he'd said. Naughty conversations with Marc had taught her that most men enjoyed a little anal play, especially with oral sex.

She wetted a finger quickly and slid it into the tight, clean hole before he could protest.

She felt his indrawn breath against her intimate flesh before he yielded and let his anus be gently probed while she sucked him.

Odette felt the hole he'd guarded open to her without a word of protest or acceptance from him. She realized that she was probably the first woman who'd been bold enough to try.

It was the first time she had done such a thing. It was an added fillip of pleasure for him, a subtle reminder that taking meant giving.

In the world of fashion, gay men often kissed each other publicly, clothed, of course, but not shy ing their appreciation for male bodies. She'd wo this aspect of it and had asked Marc.

Now, feeling naughty indeed and excited by the pleasure she'd added to for him, she withdrew her finger. She could not imagine so small a hole being violated by the cock of a male lover. No, a feminine finger was all he could handle.

For now, she wanted his cock in her mouth again. His tongue was still working her pussy with consummate skill, getting her extremely wet. Following her example, he slid a slick finger into her anus.

Odette moaned with pleasure around his cock. The gentle double penetration was stimulating her to the max.

But he was clever enough to avoid any pressure on her clitoris. She could not come. They rocked on the sofa, their heads between each other's legs, taking and giving hot oral sex, plus that little bit more for her in the ass.

Her lips stretched by the thickness of his gently thrusting shaft, she could not imagine *that* in her behind. His finger was thick enough.

He had it in nearly all the way, gliding and sliding with her natural lube. Odette clasped her stockinged legs around his back, a move that pushed her pussy up.

His finger went in her asshole to the last knuckle. He pulled his face up and stopped tongue-fucking her.

She knew he was watching his finger penetrate her behind, knew he was enjoying the moaning pleasure she was getting.

In and out. In and out.

His cock completely filled her mouth, and his balls pressed on her face as he tenderly fingerfucked her anus.

Odette cried out, experiencing an orgasm she hadn't ex-

pected. He slowly withdrew his finger from her quivering behind and wiped his wet mouth on the inside of her thigh, before
he lifted his head and got up the rest of the way.

Her nerveless fingers let go of his rock-hard cock. It was
slick and gleaming as he stood by the sofa, looking down at her.

"I didn't know I could come that way," she gasped.

"Happens," he grinned.

Odette rolled back and forth, savoring the last waves of
erotic sensation. "Never before. Not like that."

"There's more to come, Odette."

She struggled to sit up. Her freed breasts bounced over the
cami top, and the black lace bra was poking her. "I want to be
naked."

"How about almost? The stockings and the garters make
me hot. Lose the stuff on top. But not those."

"*Bien.* Help me, please."

He bent over and unhooked the bra, removing it with the cami
in a tangled, sweat-soaked mess of black. That joined the rest of
the clothes on the floor. "*Où est la salle de bain, s'il vous plaît?*"

She giggled at his guidebook French, and pointed.

"I'm coming back with hot towels," he said as he headed
that way. "One for you and one for me."

Odette lay back again to rest as she heard the water running.
A trace of fragrant steam wafted out, tickling her nose. And
then she heard the sound of the bidet. She figured he was dis-
creetly washing his asshole.

He reappeared, looking like a personal trainer—a naked personal trainer—carrying a short stack of dry towels, with two
twisted wet towels balanced on top, and a twisted washcloth.

Without ceremony, he sat down next to her and mopped her
muff. Odette laughed with pleasure. The hot, wet towel felt incredibly good and she hadn't even been fucked yet.

He grabbed her ankles and did her rear end as if she was a baby. Then he whipped a dry towel under her before he set her back down. Odette took the wet one and cleaned the finger that had gone where no woman dared to go before. Not that he wasn't clean to begin with there.

He blushed and she really laughed, handing him the towel to roll up in a dry one. "Got you, *chéri.*"

"I got you back," he muttered. "So hah." He took the wet washcloth and patted the sex sweat and the last traces of her make-up from her face, taking his time. "Think you could get used to being babied?"

"Ah, it is delicious. Now what?" She cast a meaningful look at his erection, which showed no signs of going down.

He pushed all the towels onto the floor. "I hope you have a housekeeper."

"I do."

He stood up and bent down again in a second to scoop Odette up into his arms. "I hope she doesn't like to get an early start. What the hell time is it, anyway?"

"Around three, I think." She squinted at an antique clock. "That clock is never right."

"The night is young." He kissed her on the nose and she kicked her feet. "To the bedroom."

Odette got busy kissing his shoulders and his chest, loving the feeling of being cradled in such strong arms. He carried her as if she weighed nothing. It was a good thing the hallway was long. She didn't kick, avoiding the paintings on the walls. A few were flea market finds, a few were worth a great deal. She treasured them all.

He didn't even look at them, just stopped at the open door of her bedroom before entering, and setting her down as if he were Prince Charming himself.

That is, if Prince Charming had been crossed with a handsome young satyr with a massive, swaying erection.

Odette stretched languorously on her bed, inviting him with her body to join her there.

In another moment, he did. Bryan didn't hold back, pressing the length of his body to hers, kissing her wildly.

His strength was more evident in this more natural position, where he could move as he wished.

One muscular thigh forced hers to open and his cock pushed urgently against the softness of her belly. The come he'd held back leaked a little from the head, smearing sensual heat into her skin and sticking them together for a little while in a place or two.

Her tousled hair got into her mouth, and his big hands pushed it away. For a moment, he was gentle, looking down at her, about to kiss her but somehow not ready.

His gaze was serious and highly intelligent. Odette thought with wonder and a measure of fear that she could very well love him.

Not now. Not yet. But the thought made her mind spin. In another minute, he would enter her body . . . and she knew that the connection would be more than sexual.

Sex with him was fantastic, would be even more erotic and intense face to face, but it would not be as strong as the emotions which assailed her when she looked into his eyes.

Was she alone in feeling as she did? She did not know Bryan well enough to read him accurately, if at all.

For another long moment, they looked at each as warily as animals. Then his passion dissolved his reserve, and he claimed her mouth in a hard, bruising kiss.

"Condoms in the drawer," she said breathlessly when he finally let her go. He'd thrust wildly into her belly while he'd kissed her. She wasn't going to go without that.

Bryan rose, yanked open the drawer of another Victorian

46

table set beside the bed, and rip-roll-slide, sheathed himself just like that. Covered in latex, his cock got stiffer, the thick base pumped from the tighter ring at the bottom of the condom.

How excellent that extra thickness would feel when he was all the way inside her, Odette thought dreamily. She loved the satisfying feeling of her labia stretching to accommodate a well-endowed man who filled her completely.

"On all fours," he said. "I want to get deep."

Odette made a murmur of protest—she'd wanted to see his face—then rolled over and got on hands and knees. A hard fucking from behind was something she adored.

Her own face buried in the pillows. Sexually anonymous and taking every inch of a man she could not see—ah, yes. They could begin that way.

"Wait a minute." He got up from the bed.

Odette looked around, staying in position.

"I want to see your face," he said, surprising her. "We can put a mirror here—" he lifted a medium-sized one right off the wall and positioned it on the table by the bed—"and you can see me behind you and I can see you. Okay?"

"You have done it," she said, pleased. "Of course it is okay."

She turned on the bed so that her face could be seen in the mirror.

"Yeah," he growled, bending his body over hers. He bit at her hair and tugged it, then nipped her ear.

Odette winced with pleasure.

"I love to see you react. Missed that with my head where it was."

"Couldn't be helped," she gasped. His teeth now held a hank of her hair.

Bryan let go. His eyes on her face, supporting the weight of his body on one hand, he reached under with the other and began to slap her tits gently. They swayed and bounced into each other.

The sheathed cock lying along her spine twitched and throbbed.

He got to work on her nipples next, tugging at them, pulling them into hard points. Then he circled his palm over the hot tips.

"Ahh," Odette moaned. "Put your weight on me. Use both hands."

"You sure?" he asked into her sensitive ear.

"Yes. I can take it. I love rough play on my nipples. I love you dominant like this."

She closed her eyes as she felt the coiling pressure of his body shift. He was only slightly heavier and she realized he was still holding himself up by tensing the massive muscles in his thighs.

But now he had both hands free and her breasts craved his touch.

The firm flesh filled his palms and he squeezed softly, cupping and caressing as he nipped and kissed her neck.

She felt utterly wanton, a she-animal ready to cede control to a male in a wild mood. She let her head drop a little lower and her hair slid off her nape, baring it for his love bites.

Feeling the hot cock rubbing on her back was sweet torture. The second he positioned himself to take her pussy she would not breathe.

Bryan slid back several inches, letting go of her breasts after several final slaps.

She lifted her head but she couldn't see him in the mirror. He was directly behind her, crouching down—and then his tongue slid into her pussy. His hands spread her buttocks so he could go extremely deep with every thrust.

Soft and searching, his tongue prepared her for the cock she craved. Bryan stopped for a moment to let go of her behind and spread her labia completely apart.

Odette glimpsed herself through her tumbled hair. Her open

mouth moaned with anticipation, as pink inside as the pussy he studied. Then she saw him rise behind her.

Her eyes widened when she felt the round, very firm head of his cock settle between the swollen folds of her most intimate flesh.

Bryan pushed the head just inside. "Don't move," he said. "Not one inch. Just hold me and wait."

Her whole body was trembling but she stilled when his big hands caressed her back with long, soothing strokes.

"You'll get what you want," he said softly. "All of it. So deep you won't want to move."

He inadvertently gave her the next half-inch, just under the head, when he moved forward to gather up her hair.

"Now you can see. We can both see."

She kept her eyes fixed on his reflection. His expression was taut with hot desire and the effort of self-restraint. Greedy for what he'd been giving her, she hadn't given much thought to how he'd managed to wait this long.

One hand held her hip, one hand clasped her hair. His dark eyes were shadowed with lust. Very naked, very male lust.

He dragged her back to take his first, mighty thrust and Odette cried out with erotic joy, pinned to his body by his huge cock. His balls were almost too tight to sway against her. She pressed her thighs together, trying to feel them.

Ahh. There they were, a comforting, hard-soft roundness at the base of his cock. Primed to pump out scalding-hot come that would fill the condom's tip.

Odette wriggled blissfully against his balls, forgetting about the mirror for a moment. But only for a moment. She looked into it to see him looking down at her squirming behind.

Bryan's face was drawn into hard lines, but his lips were slightly parted as he watched her succulent cheeks jiggle and push into his groin.

Her mouth opened in an O as he raised his hand above them. Down it came and she took the stinging slap, crying out. "Oh! More!"

Bryan kept his cock inside her, not thrusting, but obviously relishing the pussy reaction to the spanking he was administering. His capable hand left sensations she could feel but not see as he reddened her ass for her.

The pleasure of spanking combined with deep, motionless penetration brought a heady rush of scarlet to her cheeks as well. And having her hair held—he controlled her whole body but only to give her the most outrageous pleasure.

Her eyes glowed with shamelessness as she took the bare-bottom discipline she so much enjoyed, marveling that she had never even asked for it.

He stopped. She looked at his face in the mirror. His eyes were closed and he was swaying slightly, overcome by the power of his own desire.

"More?" she asked in a tiny voice.

"No." He opened his eyes and met her gaze. "I can't take it. I'll shoot my wad in another second if I don't stop."

He took several deep breaths and she held perfectly still on all fours.

Bryan twined his fingers more tightly in her hair, and began to thrust at last. He was so long he had to be careful, but she maneuvered herself to accommodate him.

He got wild, letting go of her hair and grabbing her hips, dragging her back for every rock forward. Her breasts bounced just from that. The sight made him wilder.

At last he stopped again, gasping, still inside her.

She arched her back in a catlike way, and he covered the curve with his body, then pulled her up with one mighty arm.

Mon Dieu. That endless cock stayed in.

"Touch yourself," he growled into her ear. His strong fingers spread out across her belly to hold her up and in place.

She finger-flicked her clit, loving that she could see his huge balls in the mirror and his thighs, classic columns of pure muscle to either side of them.

Naked, he was heroic. His hair was as messy as hers but might well have belonged to a god of long ago, spilling over his shoulders and mingling with hers.

Both hands moved up over his breasts and he pulled her upper body back hard against.

"Pull on your clit," he murmured. "Make it feel good."

His cock thrust up so far inside that she felt completely secure. With slow, steady movements, she brought herself to the verge of orgasm.

And Bryan knew it instinctively.

"Go for it," he murmured, his voice raw with desire. "I can see your face when you come . . . and your whole body . . . be inside you . . . please, Odette . . ."

"Ahh," she moaned, closer still.

"Do it for me," he whispered.

Something about the tenderness in his voice melted her last shred of resistance. She climaxed in his arms, sobbing with pleasure, knowing that he saw every second of her release. He held her only a little longer, then let her down gently to the bed.

Bryan topped her then, smoothing her hair back with careful hands, kissing her eyelids. She didn't need to see him—he was as close to her as her own soul at that moment.

Again he entered and she could tell from the extraordinary tenseness of his body that he was within seconds of a long-delayed orgasm. Delayed for her.

He thrust deeply, again and again, making a sound that had gone beyond a growl to a roar. He didn't quit, couldn't quit. At the penultimate moment, only the condom kept his explosive release contained. He reached down to hold it on, circling the rim and squeezing as he moaned in joyful agony.

She wished dreamily that they wouldn't need it some day, a falling-through-time kind of dream that she wasn't about to share. Odette stroked his shuddering back until his breaths came steadily, then ran her fingers through his hair.

"That was crazy," he whispered, "in the most beautiful way. Do you know what I mean, Odette?"

"I think so," she murmured. She didn't want to let go of him. Ever.

3

They cuddled blissfully until awakened by the singing of birds.

"Tell those damn birds to shut the hell up," Bryan said drowsily. "I don't know the French for it."

Nestled against his side, Odette smiled as best she could with her face pressed against the silky-soft skin over his ribs. The rise and fall of his chest as he breathed in his sleep had put her to sleep soon after he'd collapsed onto the bed, rolling off her but not before giving her extravagant, somewhat incoherent compliments on her beauty and sexuality and so forth. She'd understood, listening as she unsnapped her garters, unrolled her stocking and flung them into a corner.

She was surprised they'd stayed on so long.

"I'll make some coffee," she whispered, rising from the bed and heading for the kitchen.

She put the kettle on and spooned Ethiopian coffee into the press. It wouldn't be wasted on him. If all they had together were a few days, he still deserved the best.

Odette hummed as she planned a light breakfast, amused by being so domestic. She wasn't as a rule.

Of course living in Paris made it easy to pass oneself off as a great cook. She texted an order to the local gourmet grocery, and the bakery, and *voilà*, half an hour later, both orders were outside her door, delivered by the silent assistant to the concierge.

She arranged the brioche, jam, and fruit on her best plate, and maneuvered it onto a tray with the coffee press, cream, sugar, and cups. Then she hoisted the tray and headed back to her bedroom.

Bryan was sprawled across most of the bed, the sheet pulled halfway up his chest, a hand over his heart, his arm flung backward over the pillow his head rested on. He looked like he was dancing through a dream.

She would never know, because she wouldn't ask. Dreams seemed too intimate to share. And the waking ones were simply foolish.

Odette could not shake her lingering one about never letting him go. He was heading back to the U.S., he had a life there that she knew nothing about, and they would not be together.

Which made a morning like this that much sweeter.

Bryan stirred in his sleep, and she touched him gently.

"Wake up," she said. Odette didn't know if he had to be anywhere but she did. The day after a launch show was usually crowded with calls and appointments and fashion buyers.

She could only dodge her responsibilities for so long. Marc would leave her alone and make excuses, but Lucie would take a taxi and bang on the door of her apartment eventually.

"Mmm," he mumbled. "Do I smell coffee?"

"You do."

"Okay."

He opened his eyes and gave her a sleepy look that held warm passion.

Odette told herself that it was to be expected. Sex like that was uncommon—they had sparked a veritable fire in each other. But it was only sex, when all was said and done.

She poured out a cup of coffee and put it on the table by the bed.

Bryan yawned—a big, body-stretching, lionesque yawn. She remembered his roars and smiled, patting the dark fur on his chest. He turned his head to look at the cup, then at her. "Thanks."

He sat up, running a hand through hair that spiked every which way. She poured a cup for herself and looked at him, laughing between sips.

"I look that bad, huh?"

"You are adorable."

He pondered the word. "As a red-blooded American male, I don't think the word adorable can be used to describe me."

She gave a very French shrug. "Then make up your own compliment."

"I look rugged. I look sexy. I look like Brad Pitt."

Odette made a polite little grimace. "He is very pretty, but he will always look like a boy. I don't think you ever did."

Bryan smirked, putting a liberal dose of cream and sugar into his coffee. "Okay, now you're talking." He tossed the coffee down and held out his cup. "More, please."

Odette poured him another.

"You, however, are adorable. And sensual. And gorgeous. I could be in love. I feel really different." He studied her.

Odette nearly choked. Not that word. Every time she'd heard it from a man, something awful happened. They turned out to be actually in love with someone else. Or they hadn't been in love at all.

It was a very powerful word and ought to be kept locked up in a vault, as far as she was concerned.

"We hardly know each other," she said after a while. "But it is true—there are feelings—" She met his gaze with a calm look. "They are hard to define," she said.

Bryan looked disappointed. "Guess I shouldn't rush you."

"Not when you are leaving France in two days."

"Oh, right. Forgot about that. You could make me forget a lot of things, Odette."

"Pah." She waved at the tray. "Eat something. Food is better than romance."

"Is it?" He gave her a disbelieving look.

Odette tore off a piece of fresh brioche, dabbed it with strawberry jam, and put it to his lips. Bryan ate it with a look of dawning bliss.

"Hmm. You could be right." He did the same thing for her, but the piece was bigger and the jam dripped. He caught it with a finger and put it in her mouth. Odette licked it up. "So where are you off to? Back to the panty palace?"

"Do you mean the showroom? No."

"Not working today?"

"I am trying to think of a valid excuse to not go in."

"Do they need you around all the time?" he asked.

Odette made a vague gesture with her hand. "Usually."

"I guess someone has to fold the underwear," he mused. "I mean, I never go into that kind of store, outside of the occasional Valentine's Day run."

"Do you want some outfits to take home?" she asked lightly.

"Now, that is a leading question if ever I heard one," he said. He claimed the last chunk of sweet, soft, buttery brioche since she didn't seem to want it. "I don't have a girlfriend at the moment."

"Ah."

He sat up straighter, the tan skin of his muscular arms heightened by the white sheet. "Are you going to ask why?"

"No."

"I travel too much, that's why," he sighed. "But at heart, I'm a one-woman man." He made a face. "Sorry. I didn't mean to talk like a country-and-western song."

"I beg your pardon?"

"There has to be a country song about a one-woman man sick of one-night stands, but I'm damned if I can remember it."

"That is probably a good thing." She didn't know or care about country music, but she was miffed by the reference to one-night stands.

Bryan folded his arms behind his head, finished with the coffee and the brioche. She picked at the fruit.

"What's on your mind?"

"Nothing," she said, nibbling on a piece of cut pineapple. It was much too acid and she put it to one side on the tray. "I will take this away if you are done."

He reached out and took her wrist. "Hey, I didn't say thank you. Breakfast in bed—I can't remember the last time someone did that for me."

She hated whoever had, sight unseen.

"It was delicious," he was saying. "And if you're not doing anything today, can I have the honor of taking you somewhere in Paris? You have to tell me where you want to go—I'd probably take you to some tourist trap."

He meant well, but Odette was still miffed. Mornings after were always tricky. But then she almost never brought a lover home. In someone's else apartment, one had the option of leaving before daybreak.

At home—well, here she was with a virile young American who had gotten closer to her in twenty-four hours than any other man she'd ever known.

That was probably because he *was* going away, she told herself. She'd let down her guard, knowing she would not have to see him again after Friday. Which had helped her dodge the issue of telling him who she really was: not a stylist, but the multi-millionaire owner of an international lingerie company.

"Let me call Lucie at the office," she said. She glanced at the bedside clock. "*Zut.* That one is right. It is earlier than I thought. No one will be there until ten."

"All right," Bryan said happily. "Come on back to bed."

Odette could not very well refuse. She rose and picked up the tray, though, and put it on top of the dresser. Then she went back to the bed and crawled under the covers he flung back for her to her new favorite place in the whole wide world: under his arm.

She scolded herself for being so romantic but Bryan Bachman made it hard to be anything else.

Besides, she loved to nestle and he was so big and warm.

"You never did tell me how you happened to be at the back of the showroom," he began. "I couldn't believe my luck. I thought I'd seen you behind the curtains—"

"*Oui.* That was me."

"Talk directly into the nipple," he teased her. Her mouth had brushed it. "Can't quite hear you."

"It was me!"

He laughed. "I was right. And were you looking at me?"

"I was looking at the audience. You were right in front. Do you know what people will do to get a seat like yours?" she asked him.

"No. Is it that big a deal?"

"They scheme, and they pull strings, and they offer you heaps of money."

"Anyone ever do that to you?"

"I don't need money," she said, then realized her mistake. "I mean, I wouldn't want to lose my job over something like that."

"Who's the big boss?" he asked absent-mindedly. "Aren't designers supposed to come out and take bows?"

"Some do, some don't. These days fashion is more of a business than ever. The pretenders come and go."

"How'd you get into it?" She brushed her lips against his ribs, tickling him with nibbly little kisses to distract him. "Feels good, Odette. Be careful."

"I went to design school for fashion. And my mother was in the business."

"Really? As a designer?"

"No. She did embroidery. They are called the *petite mains*. The little hands. They do the detail work for the couture houses. Buttons. Faux flowers. Feather trims."

"Interesting."

"It is painstaking work, and they are true artisans. But their craft is dying. Most of the women are old now and nobody young wants to do the work."

"Do you know how?"

Odette nodded. "It is useful for a stylist. But no, I would not want to make my living at it."

Her conscience pricked her. Tell him the truth, it said. Your house supports a dozen such craftswomen, who will be able to retire in comfort. And you have vowed to keep alive their artisan skills as well.

It was only one of her pet causes. How much money did one woman need? Giving it away was fun.

He might find her charity noble—he did not seem to be aware that the ticket he'd bought had benefited it. But then it had been worded in French, and no doubt the young girl who'd sold it to him had wanted to talk about *Le O.C.* once she'd seen his tank top, which said Newport Beach in big white letters.

But the uncomfortable issue of why she had not told him the truth in the first place was sure to come up.

Bryan Bachman had turned out to be intelligent and passionate and . . . incredibly sexual. He would not be flattered to find out that she'd chosen him for a fling. Unluckily for her, he was the kind of man who wanted more, although he was honest enough about his footloose status.

The thing was . . . she wanted him to come back. If it was possible. If he wanted to. If not, then good-bye and good luck. He would likely never find out, because it was not as if he cared about fashion or the crazy people who made their living at it.

And he would not be a wanderer for long.

Such were her thoughts until he prodded her. "Can you get me behind the scenes?"

Odette raised her head, and propped her flushed cheek on one hand. "Why on earth? Wasn't that show enough for you? You said it gave you a headache."

"I said the music gave me a headache. Okay, the models were too skinny, but the Arelquin women were a lot of fun to talk to."

"Your charms were not lost on either of them," she said wryly.

"Huh?"

"Never mind."

"Anyway, it would be something to do. If you don't have to work, that is."

"My female intuition tells me that you have an ulterior motive, Bryan."

He guffawed. "You're good. You're very good. I do."

Odette felt her stomach sink. "What is it?"

"My mother was a dressmaker. Didn't I tell you that?"

"If you did, I don't remember it," she said cautiously.

"Not hot couture or whatever you call it."

"*Haute* couture."

"Whatever. She made prom dresses and bridal gowns and things like that. We got by."

Odette had to ask. "What happened to your father?"

"He took off to grow pot in Mendocino. Never paid a nickel of child support and never sent a postcard. I didn't know him, so I didn't miss him. No, it was just me and Mom."

Odette couldn't resist. "Her style sense did not rub off on you."

"I'm a guy. What do you want from me?"

"I don't know." She patted his bare chest, feeling suddenly wistful. "But naked, you are *magnifique*. And not very many people can say that. Which is why clothing designers make so much money sometimes."

"Yeah, well, never mind that," he said cheerfully. "You French are very interested in everyone's family. Madame Arelquin asked me the same question about my father."

"And did you give her the same answer?"

"I said he was a hippie and let it go at that."

"What did she say?"

Bryan grinned as he tried to remember it exactly. "She looked very sad. She said it was too bad that my *maman* had to marry an eepee and not a nice bankaire."

"That sounds like her."

"Anyway, my mother would be thrilled with a virtual tour of a real Paris fashion house."

Odette knew she had just painted herself in a corner. "But they are very secretive. No one is allowed to see a collection before it is shown. Designs are knocked off within hours in countries where labor is cheap."

"I can imagine," he said easily. "Well, it was just a thought."

"I'll see what I can do," she said. There must be a way to get him in somewhere else. Not that the nearly naked fitting models who hung around Oh! Oh! Odette catching up on gossip and knitting would care if a stranger strolled through.

And what had he said? That they were too skinny for him? Odette was finding more and more reasons to fall for him.

He sighed with happiness. "Guess I'd better get going." He pushed back the covers and got up, fluffing his stuff. "Mind if I take a shower?"

"Of course not. So long as I can join you."

"All right. You get it going and I'll be right there."

It was as good an opportunity as any to end a conversation that was likely to trip her up. Odette headed for the bathroom, and set out scented soaps and great big towels.

With the water running, she couldn't hear anything, and came out to look for him.

Completely naked and unselfconscious, Bryan was looking at the art in her hallway. He looked without much interest at the graffiti-influenced Basquiat painting that she'd bought in New York, and then moved from framed photograph to photograph, studying the images.

"These are by Henri Cartier-Bresson."

"Yes," she said quietly. She was surprised that he would know that, and a little ashamed of herself for being surprised. He was educated and not uncultured. But the photographer's signatures on the original prints were small and not that easy to read, and only one image was well-known. The others were lesser works that showed men and women, not posed, at a moment of connection—or coming apart.

She was curious to know what he thought of them—not all were pretty and a few were heartbreaking. Odette had bought them when the great photographer died because each one spoke to her in silence and she saw something new each time she looked at them.

And now Bryan, this man she scarcely knew, was looking at

them in the quiet of the morning. She felt suddenly frightened, as if he were looking into her heart. His own silence upset her, but she scolded herself for it.

He was entitled to look at them—that was why she had put them on the walls. And yet, no one but him ever had.

"Someone said Cartier-Bresson photographs the moment after the last word is spoken," Odette said at last.

"Someone got that right."

He came back to bed, the strong planes of his body outlined by the morning light and softened by the opaque shadows it cast at the same time. She'd peeked outside the bathroom window. It was going to rain. No wonder they'd slept so peacefully. She always did on rainy days.

It couldn't just be him.

4

Odette had called in and found out she had to go to work. Bryan was on his own. The day had dawned overcast, according to the pictogram on the front page of a French newspaper he'd glanced at when he'd left her neighborhood, not that he'd noticed that under the covers with her. Her shutters had been closed while they had breakfast in bed.

And the weather was going to get worse. The unmoving clouds were only getting darker. He didn't want to go back to his depressing hotel and he couldn't just camp out at her place like he was moving in. Uncool, no matter what country you were in.

And, he thought ruefully, she hadn't begged him to stay. But they'd made plans to meet up in the evening at a place called Chez Prune on the Canal St. Martin.

She'd said his outfit was fine. She'd even bestowed a pair of men's underwear on him, a prototype pair of briefs that were comfortable but *really* brief.

Even wearing the rest of yesterday's clothes, he wasn't too disgusting. She'd scrubbed him thoroughly and playfully in the shower and they'd had a squeaky-clean quickie on the gigantic bathmat. Her bathroom alone was about as big as his Newport Beach studio apartment.

He had a feeling that was unusual in Paris, which was a really pricey place to live. Her neighborhood seemed more quiet than expensive, but he was no judge of that.

The buildings breathed distinction that had to do with their age, he guessed. He'd glanced at the plaque and seen 1656, then a lot of historical information in French he hadn't stopped to read.

Her place was nice, though. He liked the eclectic mix of things and her style in general. She was in the right business, he thought, feeling a little more cheerful. His mom would love Odette.

Yeah. He told himself to get real. His mom was never going to meet Odette. He had two days, more or less, to share with a hot French chick who was more than nice to him and was wild, really wild, in the sack.

Why couldn't he just be grateful for that? His days of being dumbstruck by puppy love were behind him, and he was—would be, he corrected himself—looking for something more.

The real deal. Whatever the hell that was. Sure could be easy to confuse red-hot sex with it. He went on his way, walking easily over cobblestone streets that were probably ancient.

He ought to bone up on French history, impress her a little. *Vive la France* and all that.

It was a great city and he wished he had more time. Sure, he could always fly back and look her up—speaking of that, he ought to check his flight.

And his e-mail. Maybe the interviewer from *Bonjour Paris* had forwarded the jpegs. It would be cool if Odette appeared in them somewhere. He'd love a memento like that. How We Met.

He scowled at his corny impulse to commemorate a relationship that was going to be over soon. But he went into the first internet café he saw.

He could use more coffee.

A few minutes later, he had a thick cup of zhoe, as the girl behind the counter, who'd worked as an au pair in Chicago, called it. And it was damn good zhoe, too. Hot and strong.

He booted up the computer in the corner, where he could look out on the street if he wanted to, and be left alone. He pulled up his Hotmail traveling account, and waited idly while the new messages loaded.

The attachment icon showed next to one from *Bonjour Paris.* Aww. She'd come through, or the bald photographer in bad-ass black leather had.

He clicked and clicked but he couldn't get the attachment to open. Bryan swore under his breath. He couldn't even figure out a different program to open them with.

Fuck.

He scrolled the other messages. Nothing from the universities he'd applied to, nothing from friends. Just the usual weird shit that had escaped the spam filter, offers to extend his dick and the like.

Odette did a fine job of that, he thought with a grin. He blew on his coffee and shifted his leg to hide the I-heart-Odette hard-on he was getting, in case the counter girl looked his way.

Bryan decided to check out the *Bonjour Paris* website. There had to be photos on it, and the lingerie show had looked like a big deal. Maybe there wouldn't be any of him, but then again, he told himself smugly, he had been the winner of a quote-unquote coveted front-row seat.

He was just sitting here. Might as well take an ego trip.

The site downloaded quickly and photos of the leggy babes

in underwear and their fine feathers came up first. Then the headline. *Oh! Oh! Odette!*

Bryan sat up straight, forgetting all about his coffee. He couldn't read the text in French that well, but a few facts jumped out at him from what he suspected was breathless gush. Odette Gaillard, youngest CEO in France. Odette Gaillard, ex-model. Odette Gaillard, multimillionaire. Odette Gaillard, bad girl gone good.

She wasn't a stylist. She owned the fucking business. She was a self-made woman, not even thirty, obviously talented, and an A-list guest all over the world. She had to know dozens of rich guys and movie stars. What did she see in him? Why hadn't she told him who she really was?

She must not have wanted him to know any of that. She must have been looking for a fast fling when she'd seen him, and told her assistants to keep away while she tried her luck.

He had to admit that doing it that way leveled the playing field some. He'd gone with her because he thought she was hot. And really nice. And the thrift-store outfit had fooled him.

Wherever she got those crazy clothes, they were not from a thrift store. Or a flea market. They were designer items made to look like thrift store duds.

Bryan wanted to bang his fist on the counter. Instead he just sat there staring at underwear models like a perv, not even seeing them, until he realized the girl at the counter was giving him a disgusted look.

He clicked out of the site. His mind was whirling. Okay, so now what? They were going to meet tonight, and what would he do if she kept on pretending she was just a poor little stylist?

With an amazing apartment in an exclusive *arrondissement,* you dickbrain.

He sighed and looked it up online.

Yes indeed, Odette's quiet neighborhood was populated by

tech-biz billionaires who kept models for pets. And freaky sheiks who had been sent off to France by their exasperated families with suitcases full of petrodollars. Her neighborhood didn't breathe distinction or age, it breathed money. As in mega-money.

Her concept furniture, rose-embedded Lucite armchair and all, had probably cost a fortune and so did the original photographic prints signed by the greatest master of the art.

Henri Cartier-Bresson *was* his favorite photographer. Odette must have thought he was making that up, along with his degree in marine biology. Not like he could sit around and talk ocean currents with her, right?

Good thing he hadn't commented on the oddball paintings on the wall—she would have laughed.

Did he get to ask questions from here on in? Now that he thought of it, she'd deflected quite a few so expertly he hadn't known she was shining him on.

Bryan looked down at his Newport Beach tank and neoprene jacket. Clothes made the man. She must have taken him for a studly surfer, and figured he had the brains of a boogie board. But he couldn't forget the way she'd looked at him, clothed and naked . . . like he meant something to her.

Yeah. Sure he did. A fresh entry in her Filofax under *M* for *Men.* No, make that *H* for *Hommes.* Beach boy, American, subspecies, California. How many stars would she give him for the sex? One for each of their three days. Over and out.

Bryan was crushed just thinking about it. He turned around when he heard the clatter of cups and realized that the first girl was going off her shift, and a new one was just starting. Serious-looking, thick glasses, and was that a copy of Simone de Beauvoir's essays she'd just set on the counter?

Yup. She would make a point of ignoring him.

Bryan opened up the *Bonjour Paris* website again, looking

for more photos. Hell. There he was, grinning like a fool. That witchy interviewer had practically stuck the mike up his nose while he answered questions he only half-understood.

Smile and wave. He was waving to his mom. But he didn't look too bright doing it. He photographed okay. No wonder the rich and powerful Odette Gaillard had mistaken him for a California gigolo with sand in his flip-flops. Weird that she'd wanted him anyway.

Christ. Was his name in the captions? What if the graduate admissions officers looked him up on Google and laughed their fucking heads off? No, he hadn't broken any laws or revealed any personal parts, but if they had to chose between Joe Nerd and Beach Blanket Bozo, all other things being equal, they would chose Joe Nerd and not him.

He scrolled through all the photos and peered at the text. The interviewer had spelled Bryan as Brian and Bachman as Backmann. He was safe. He really couldn't be angry with Odette. She'd had no way of knowing anything about him, and she'd only wanted to protect herself. That was understandable.

And she'd wanted him, gone out of her way to talk to him. Something he found even more flattering. Being taken for a boy toy by a hot, sophisticated Frenchwoman wasn't the worst thing that had ever happened to him.

He didn't have to mention the encounter when he e-mailed his mother. Gloria Bachman would be thrilled to hear that he'd won a ticket to an honest-to-God runway show. He'd send her the link to the website; she'd enjoy the pictures. She was that kind of mother. No matter what he got himself into, his mom kept right on thinking he walked on water.

Now, if there was some way he could take her on a virtual tour of a Paris fashion house . . . Odette could help with that.

No, he wasn't going to guilt-trip her into it. Bryan had no idea how to even tell her that he knew who she really was.

The more he thought about it, the more he remembered how she'd looked when she came up to him at the back of the showroom, ignoring all the craziness onstage, and the glamorous crowd.

Almost like she didn't want to be there either.

No one had recognized her when they'd gone clubbing—she'd blended into the raffish crowd like she belonged anywhere she wanted to be, drinking and dancing and living it up.

And after they'd ended up at her place, she'd really let down her hair. He would never, ever forget how they hit the heights of lust and came down again—or afterward. Odette had cuddled up to him like a stray cat who'd just found a friend.

It was strange, considering who she was, but he wouldn't have changed a thing about their first encounter.

Bryan wondered if she would confess before Friday. Fuck it. He didn't care. Rule one: life didn't follow the rules.

He glanced at the street outside. The city looked rainwashed and sad, its workaday aspect revealed in the hurrying passers-by shielding themselves with umbrellas or folded newspapers. He wondered where Odette was and what she was doing.

Odette had entered her atelier later than usual, dressed more soberly than usual. She couldn't wear sunglasses, not on a rainy day, and hide from the inquisitive stares. What had happened between her and Bryan Bachman was nobody's business but hers.

But gossip traveled fast. She'd made herself conspicuous by disappearing and not taking the customary bow at the show's grand finale. Well, she wasn't going to take any questions about it.

"*Bonjour,*" she said to no one in particular, playing the role of lady boss as she strode by workstations cluttered with projects in various stages of development.

Marc popped his head out of his office to wink at her, but he didn't say a word. Odette breathed a sigh of relief.

"The show went well, Madame." Lucie bustled up before Odette could disappear into her own sanctuary. "Today the Japanese buyers are coming in. Their Harajuku flagship store is placing a big order."

Odette gave a start. She'd forgotten about the meeting. That order ran into the millions. The Japanese loved French designer goods.

"Do they want the line we showed?"

Lucie sniffed. "Of course not. They insist on exclusivity."

"Then we will use the new patterns as templates and tweak the fabrics and trim," Odette sighed. "There is no time to create a completely exclusive line for them, not if we are to meet our loan obligations. We need that order, Lucie."

Making millions meant borrowing millions. Her personal fortune was secure, apart from what she'd plowed back into the company, but the banks insisted on growth projections that she could not guarantee. Fashion was a risky business, even with a popular brand sold worldwide.

"Yes, we do." Lucie made a few notes on her clipboard and bustled elsewhere.

Odette headed for her office. The sloping windows of the old atelier rose from the top of the wall in back of her desk to the point of the roof. On a fine day, they let in so much light that shades had to be drawn against it. On a gray day, the light was muted, almost sad.

Odette switched on her desk light, needing the touch of glowing scarlet that its beaded silk shade provided.

Her assistant came in. She could guess what Marc was going to ask. She was almost surprised he'd been able to wait five minutes.

Odette looked up at him and smiled.

"So," Marc said nonchalantly, "how did your enchanted evening go? I didn't tell anyone why you left."

"They seemed to have figured it out. Did you take a bow for me?"

"Yes. The crowd called for you, though, when they saw the white satin set trimmed with real pearls—*oo là là.* The bride at the finale got a lot of applause."

"Brides always do."

"Yes. Did you have fun with with M'sieu Neoprene?"

"His name is Bryan Bachman. He is very nice," Odette said primly.

"Ah. So nice you stayed up until dawn."

"Not quite. The birds woke us up a little late."

"How romantic. Breakfast in bed for two?" he purred.

"Yes, as a matter of fact."

"I'm jealous. You look weary but beautiful."

"I had no time to put on makeup, Marc. Take me as I am."

He folded his arms across his chest. "I approve. You should go out with him again."

"Why do you say that?"

She flipped open a ring binder packed with sales figures, sales projections, client comments, sketches, and everything else she could cram into it, flipping the pages with the eraser end of her pencil.

"Because you work too hard, Odette. You need someone like him. A real California beach boy."

"He is not a boy."

Marc raised his eyebrows. "It is only a phrase. How old is he?"

"Twenty-five, I think. Or twenty-six. I cannot remember if I asked or what he said. That is my best guess."

"And he is not from the beach?"

"He grew up near there. He has a degree in marine biology and he wishes to go to graduate school."

Marc looked pleased. "A smart beach boy. Even better."

"Too smart, perhaps," she muttered. "Please, Marc. I have work to do."

"Of course. I just wanted to satisfy my curiosity. And by the way—the fitting model will be in at noon. She called to say that she was throwing up."

Odette made a face. "Disgusting. I wish they would not do that."

"It is unfortunate. Should I have Lucie order coffee for you? Ah, no—you mentioned having breakfast."

She smirked. "Yes. But thank you."

Marc gave a nod and left her office.

Odette leaned back in her chair and looked up at the gloomy sky overhead. Then she glanced at her binder, not eager to immerse herself in spreadsheets. Fashion was no longer fun or creative. It was numbers-driven. Clients were nervous sheep, who wanted a sure thing they had never seen before.

There were times when she wondered if she should leave the business.

She put down her pencil and put her head in her hands, feeling a headache coming on. Odette reminded herself of how many people she employed and also of her charitable commitments. Walking away from her company was not an option at the moment.

Her night with the freewheeling American seemed to have shaken her up in more ways than one.

Pah. She was too old for romantic fantasies about a man changing her life. You are almost thirty, she reminded herself. That wasn't old at all, though.

She wished she could take off and wander the world for a little while. With Bryan. Was it possible that he . . . well, what if he were to come back to Paris someday, when she was not so busy . . .

Odette felt a sickish sensation creep into her stomach. He really didn't know who she was, but he was bound to find out sooner or later. She ought to confess as soon as possible.

Being successful was not a crime. Feeling flirty and wanting an uncomplicated encounter also was not a crime.

Sex with him had been extraordinary. Her unexpected feelings for him had overwhelmed her. What a mix. Tenderness. Curiosity. Passion. Was it because she'd set aside her identity that she'd felt so free?

All he had to do was type in her name on Google to find out about her. But then again, why would he? He had no reason not to believe her. She hoped.

If it came to that, she would explain as best she could. Make it up to him. Contribute a large sum to *his* favorite charity. Save The Oysters. She supposed they needed saving, along with everything else?

No. She had a feeling he could not be bought and she could not be such a hypocrite, because she ate oysters. Raw if not kicking.

Preoccupied, Odette chewed her pencil and pored over her binder.

The Japanese buyers had come and gone by the time Odette looked at her watch. She had five minutes to get all the way to Chez Prune in north Paris and meet Bryan.

"Lucie!" she called. "I cannot work late tonight! Where are you?"

The girl scurried to her door. "Here. Go." She was holding Odette's light coat, which she thrust out to her boss, along with an umbrella. "I will close up."

"*Merci!*" Odette dashed down the winding marble staircase, swinging on the turns with one hand on the wrought iron balustrade. She dashed out the front door and looked frantically through the rain for a taxi.

There were none. Just the usual insane Paris rush-hour traffic. The streets were clogged with cars, weaving in and out, and cutting each other off. The driving rain meant everyone's windows stayed rolled up, which muffled the curses.

She would have to walk until she could hail one. She unfurled the umbrella and started off, dodging right and left to get past people. Little by little, despite her haste, she relaxed.

There was something about a rainy night in a big city that she loved. Neon reflections on dark, slick streets, open umbrellas like giant dots of color against the gray—she slowed down to take it in. She would get a taxi eventually, Bryan would wait, she should not be so frantic—*Mon Dieu,* my shoes are soaked, she thought.

After several more blocks, her luck changed and she spotted a taxi. It pulled over. She got in, sliding her furled umbrella at her feet, and gave the driver directions.

Odette felt suddenly exhilarated. Her feet were cold and wet, but Paris in the rain was beautiful as ever, and she was going to meet her new lover—

Paris in the rain . . . it could be a perfect name for her next collection.

She had been considering a new type of gray silk, pleated so finely that it shimmered. The manufacturer had made variations on that theme, deeper hues shot through with flashes of silver.

Like lights reflecting on wet streets at night, if one were looking out a café window, protected from the storm . . . with a man one loved. She smiled a little wistfully.

Paris in the rain? You can't slap a concept like that on fancy panties. On umbrellas, maybe. Not underwear. In her head, she could hear the grumpy voice of her sales analyst, a man who hated new ideas.

Zut. He might be right. Odette sighed and leaned back against the seat, grateful that the taxi driver wasn't the talkative kind.

She leaned forward and tapped on the divider. "Here it is. Thank you." She handed him the fare and a generous tip, then clambered out, forgetting the umbrella on the floor.

At the entrance to Chez Prune, Odette caught a glimpse of her reflection in the window and made an effort to pull herself together, patting her damp hair back. The long day at work and her lack of makeup showed. She certainly looked like a junior worker in a fashion house.

It didn't matter. Prune customers were arty types, usually disheveled and prone to announcing that they didn't give a damn about money, before they hit up their pals for a loan.

She looked for Bryan as she entered, not seeing him at first. Ah—there he was. His back was to her. He was wearing a heavy sweater and a different jacket was slung over the back of his chair. Of course—he must have gone back to his hotel to change.

He was alone. She was glad that no one had struck up a conversation with him—meaning no one female.

Odette knew she had no right to be jealous, but she was anyway. She came up behind him and tapped him on the shoulder.

"Hello," she said. "Have you been waiting long?"

He got up and kissed her on the cheek. "No, not long. Mad dash through the rain for you, I guess." He touched a straggling lock of her damp hair with an odd tenderness that touched her even more.

"For a little while. Then I got lucky. But guess what—"

The waiter came over, and asked what they wanted to drink.

"Calvados for me," she said.

"What's that?" Bryan asked.

"Apple brandy. It warms you up very nicely."

"I'll have that then."

"Two calvados," she told the waiter, who gave them a blasé nod and went away.

"So how was your day?" Bryan asked.

"Oh, much the same," Odette said quickly. She could not imagine how she was going to tell him the truth. But looking into his eyes, she knew she had to.

"I just sort of wandered around," he said.

"Not a good day for that."

"No. I went into a café after a while. Checked my e-mail."

"Ah. Did you tell, um, your friends about the show?" Odette looked up gratefully when the waiter returned with two glasses of apple brandy. She was going to need it. She picked up her glass and took a tiny but fortifying sip.

"Actually, no. Just my mom. The girl from *Bonjour Paris* had promised to e-mail the photos her guy took. I couldn't open them, so I pulled up the website and—"

Odette took a much bigger sip and coughed.

"There you were," he finished.

For a long moment they just looked at each other. She didn't see anger in his eyes at the way she'd misled him. But she was going to let him do the talking for the moment.

"Look, I understand why you wouldn't necessarily want me to know that you were such a big deal."

She nodded, unable to think of a thing to say. *I thought you were sexy. I wanted you. I took a chance.* All true, but too revealing.

"And if I'd been paying attention, I could have figured it out."

"The misunderstanding"—she hesitated—"was my fault, not yours."

He picked up his glass of brandy and took a healthy swig. "You know what? When I thought about it, I didn't really care. We had a great time. I made it clear that I only had a couple of days in Paris."

"Unfortunately."

"What?"

"I wish you could stay longer," she blurted out. "Forgive me for saying so."

A slight blush colored his tan. "I'm not used to this."

"And by that you mean . . ."

He shrugged. "Lust at first sight."

Odette felt an infinitesimal crack open in her heart. A forgotten part of her had been hoping that love had something to do with this. Or would have. Evidently not.

Or not where he was concerned, anyway.

"Go on," she said.

"I mean, what happened last night—was fantastic. I never had sex like that."

"No? You are a skillful lover."

He gave her a long look. "Thanks. I'm not too good at this stuff, though. Talking about it, I mean."

"We don't have to talk."

"Yeah, well . . ." He folded his arms, and looked at her steadily. "I think we should. Even if we only have another day or so, we can get to know each other."

"Ah. I suppose we could." She smiled uncertainly. The way he looked in the thick sweater, warm and masculine, made her want to jump into his lap, and start all over again. For however long. "Where should we start?"

He glanced over her shoulder at the drenched customers

who'd just come in, greeting their friends with waves that shook drops of water on their table. "Not a great time to tour Paris. The weather's going to be like this for a while. Besides, you have work to do."

"You can spend a day at my atelier, if you like," Odette offered. Would he want to? He had said his mother was a dressmaker. He might feel at home.

"I was just going to ask that." He looked relieved. "I e-mailed my mom about winning the front-row seat at your show. She wanted to know all about it. Asked if I'd met you."

Odette, made brave by the brandy, permitted herself a smile. "And what did you say?"

"I said yes, we met. Informally," he added.

Odette blew out her breath. "It is easier to lie in an e-mail."

He shook his head. "I wasn't lying. I just wasn't telling her everything."

Odette pressed her lips together, feeling guilty all over again despite his reassurance. "Fair enough. So . . . of course, yes, you can visit my atelier. Bring a camera. So long as you do not take pictures of the designs."

"Of course not. I understand why. I know what trade secrets are."

"Ah, Bryan—that is not why I didn't tell you who I was. It never occurred to me that you were anything other than who you seemed to be—"

"Shall we order?"

She looked from his handsome, open face to that of the waiter, and took the hint. The subject of how they'd met was now closed. She drew in a deep breath and took one of the two proffered menus, ordering the first thing she saw and a bottle of plonk. She handed the menu back to the waiter.

Bryan suppressed a chuckle and said he'd have the same thing, whatever it was. The waiter picked up the brandy glasses and came back with two wineglasses and a dark green bottle with no label.

"So is that plonk?"

"Yes. *Vin ordinaire.* Theirs is often good."

They made small talk and drank until the meal arrived.

"*Pot au feu.*" She whiffed the fragrant steam coming from the bowls the waiter set down. "You will like it."

"I believe in taking chances." He helped himself to a chunk of bread from the basket. "This looks like the good stuff, nice and chewy. Like what we had at your place."

"So it does." She was halfway through the bowl before she asked him to spend the night again.

They'd gotten out of the taxi several blocks before her street, because Odette had wanted to walk. The rain had stopped, but the dark streets glistened.

She was under his arm, warm and content. "It is too bad that it's raining."

"It's okay. I don't mind the rain. I like the way it makes everything look different."

Pleased by his offhand comment, she didn't say anything but pressed a light kiss on the masculine hand draped over her shoulder.

"What was that for?" he asked.

"Oh, nothing."

"You warm enough?"

"Yes."

"Paris is colder than I expected."

"A lot of people think so. It suits me. But I take my holidays in warm places."

"Did you grow up here, Odette?"

"Yes," she said. "Not in the city, though." She named the suburb. "You wouldn't know it."

"I could look it up online."

Odette gave a heartfelt sigh. "From now on, I will be honest. So just ask."

He gave her shoulders a squeeze. "I never dated anyone like you. Can we just forget about the you-rich-me-poor part?"

"For sure. Besides, I wasn't always."

"So I gathered. You did it on your own." He paused. "Wait a minute. We have to figure out how to walk together."

"Your legs are too long," she said happily.

"Sorry."

They started off again, turning a corner.

"I always wanted to go into business. You know I was a model—"

"And I'm glad you're not anymore."

"Yes," she laughed. "I like to eat. Anyway, I was done with it by twenty-five and I found a backer. I never expected the line to take off like it did, but I was very successful."

"The show was amazing."

"I have done many, but I want to branch out. Fragrances, accessories—if I can license my name, I won't have to work so hard."

"Hmm."

They had come into a passage roofed in glass where there were no cars, and no people either at this hour of the night. She made him stop in front of a chic little millinery shop. "See the flowers on those hats? My mother made things like that by hand for *couturiers*. It's a dying art. Everything is prêt-à-porter now—ready to wear and outsourced."

He looked at the display. "Yeah, my mother couldn't really compete. Not when there are warehouses stuffed with prom dresses and bridal gowns. So I get it."

"Perhaps she will visit Paris someday," Odette said. "With you."

He didn't answer, because they'd left the passage and the rain began to fall again, coming down hard out of clouds they couldn't see in the night.

"Let's go!" He grabbed her hand and they ran the rest of the way, with her in the lead, trying not to twist her ankle on the cobblestones.

They arrived at the door of her apartment building, breathless, laughing, and soaked to the skin, and raced up the marble stairs.

Odette searched for her key while they both stood shivering on the mat, jamming it into the lock.

Once inside, he took off his jacket and went to the bathroom to hang it up, pulling off his sweater on the way back. "You mind? This thing smells like a wet dog."

"Of course not. But I don't have anything to give you to wear."

"No? I was wondering if those briefs you gave me—"

"A prototype."

"I remember. I'm just giving you a hard time." He slid a hand down his jeans to adjust them. "But they need work. Back to the drawing board, Design Girl. I've been tugging my nuts all day."

She giggled. "I will make a note of that."

"So you're doing a line of men's underwear?"

"I might."

"Need a model?"

She only laughed. "You could do it, Bryan. You have a real-man look. Buff, but not too buff."

He ran a hand over his bare chest. "Would I have to get waxed?"

"Probably."

"Then forget it."

"You don't have that much chest hair, Bryan. And none at all on your back. You are just right. Anyway, Marc says that fur is back."

His hand stopped. "Who's Marc?"

"My assistant and right-hand man. He keeps me informed on trends in male fashion."

"I hope he's gay." At her nod, he grinned. "Good. I don't have to be jealous."

"He is a little jealous of me, put it that way."

"You mean he knows who I am?" Bryan asked.

"He saw you at the show. But he says things like that to make me laugh. He thinks I work too hard."

"You probably do." He came closer. "Don't you want to get out of that coat and stuff? You'll catch cold."

"*Zut.* Of course." She let him remove her coat, shrugging out of the sleeves as he helped her out of it. "You distracted me, walking around half-naked."

He turned her around and rubbed her arms with his hands. "Did I?"

Odette turned her face up to his to reply, but she didn't get a chance. In another second, he was kissing her, deeply, warmly.

She responded, caressing his chest, enjoying the way he trembled. "Cold hands," he murmured into her mouth.

Odette moved them to his waist, then over his lower back, and finally down into his jeans. She held his muscular butt while he went back to kissing her.

"I think those briefs fit you just fine," she whispered when the kiss stopped.

"I still want to take them off," he said. "But I'll do it any way you want me to."

"Inch by inch. Nice and slow."

Bryan laughed a little self-consciously. "You really know how to make a guy feel cheap."

Odette slid her hand around to the front of his jeans and got her fingers around his erection, stroking him as best she could.

She didn't have much room, not with a great big cock like his. "You have something very nice to show off, *m'sieu.*"

"Huh. Glad you like it." He looked down at her slender hand inside his jeans. "It likes you."

She pouted her lips and blew a kiss at his cock, then laughed when he twitched it. "I guess so."

"Told you. C'mon, let's get you undressed."

Odette shook her head. "I don't want to be naked yet."

"Feeling shy?"

"No. I want to take my time. Besides, it is still cold in here—I should adjust the thermostat and—"

"That just doesn't sound sexy," he sighed.

"I want to watch you do a striptease."

"Oh. *Oh.*" He gave her a hug that extended his hard-on. "That's different. Go change then. Get comfortable. Get ready for a girl's night out."

Odette sauntered down the hallway, unbuttoning the damp clothes she still wore. "For one girl. Me." She paused to reset the thermostat dial on the way.

"I wouldn't have it any other way," he called from the kitchen. Cabinet doors were opening and closing.

When she returned, she found a tray with a pitcher of drinks and two glasses. "What is this?"

"My speciality. More-or-Less Margaritas. Guaranteed to knock you on your beautiful ass."

"*Bien.*"

"Wow," he said, noticing her lingerie. "That's some gown. Your design?"

"Of course." She turned around to show him. Nearly backless, the sheer gown fit her like a second skin—and showed her real skin underneath. Lace, strategically placed, covered her nipples and soft mound, but everything else was revealed.

"Stay there," he muttered. He took a step closer, barefoot now, and she sighed with pleasure when he began to stroke her bottom with his big, warm hands, moving the sheer material of the gown underneath his palms to give her even more subtle stimulation. "Nice and silky. Do you like the way that feels?"

"Yes," she whispered. She looked over her shoulder at him. "Don't stop."

Bryan moved his hands in slow circles . . . rubbing . . . rubbing . . . still not baring her bottom. The sensation was exquisite. Her labia swelled plump and wet without him touching them at all.

"You're like a cat," he murmured. "You like lots of stroking and gentleness."

"At first."

Her eyes were half-closed and she wasn't looking over her shoulder anymore, but she could sense him smile at her reply. "Yeah. You like to get wild too," he said.

Bryan stopped what he was doing and turned her around to face him. He got her by the waist, enjoying making the sheer material slide a little over her skin there too.

Then he kissed her again, rubbing himself through his jeans. Twined around each other, they surrendered to the sweetness of foreplay, until she put a hand to his cheek and stopped him.

Looking a little dazed, Bryan took a couple of deep breaths. Odette ran her hand over the tautness of his abs, then rested her fingertips on his male nipples. She looked a little closer at the right one, seeing a small hole in it.

"Did you—" she began.

"That used to be pierced," he said.

"Ah."

"I got hit on by gay guys at the beach too much. I took it out and forgot about it."

Odette nodded. "But would you wear one for me?"

"Of course. You do have a striptease coming up."

"I have something that would fit. A little gold earring. Very plain."

"That would do it."

She patted his chest. "I'll be right back."

It took her less than a minute to find what she was looking for in her jewelry box. She came back into the room to find him pulling on his nipple, stretching the hole a little.

"May I?" she asked.

He nodded. She took his nipple between her fingertips and slid the wire of the small gold ring through it. He winced but held steady.

She stepped back. "The final touch. You are beautiful."

"Thanks. I don't think of myself like that, but thanks."

He was, though. The thick hair, like a rock star, and those sexy eyes—and *mon Dieu*, that body of his. Tall and leanly muscled. The tiny ring drew the eye to his chest, and only added to his masculine self-assurance.

"Okay. Am I ready?" he asked.

Odette settled back into the sofa. "I think so."

He bent over to pour her a drink and she reached forward, catching the ring with her fingertip. She pulled it ever so gently.

"Hmm. Easy, now. Feels good, though."

She used it to bring him even closer for a soft, brief kiss. "All right. Strip." She picked up her drink.

"Never did this."

"I don't care."

As it turned out, he was a natural. He didn't have dancer moves, but he was athletic and any move he made was sexy. He popped the steel button out of the frayed buttonhole and eased the zipper down until he could open his jeans.

Then he pushed the briefs down underneath, taking out his cock, handling himself with rough ease.

"Just look," he said.

She nodded, staring hungrily at the veined, heavy shaft in his hands.

Bryan began to stroke himself, his eyes on her. But she couldn't meet his gaze. His self-stimulation was fascinating to watch. His strong fingers slid up and down, stopping just under the plum of the head, pumping until a pearly drop appeared in its slit.

"Want that?" he asked huskily.

Odette sat forward. He guided her head and put his cock near her mouth. She liked this game. She wasn't going to suck him greedily, even though she wanted to.

No. Tip to tip. Her tongue darted out and took the drop. Then she closed her mouth.

"Exactly like a cat," he said in a low voice. "You don't do anything you don't want to do. But you like licking come, don't you?"

Odette nodded.

He pumped another drop for her, and flinched when she took longer about licking it. She got her tongue tip into the slit and cleaned it nicely for him. Bryan gritted his teeth. "Uhh. Yeah. So ladylike. You're driving me crazy."

Odette sat back again. "Take those jeans off." She curled her feet under her, and sleeked the sheer gown over her thighs, picking up her drink. Salty man and sweet lime were a delicious combination. She ran her tongue over her lips as he slid the jeans down.

Inch by inch. He reached his hands over his head when the jeans and briefs together were down far enough to release his balls too, and gave her a slow dance, letting her feast her eyes on all of it.

Aroused, he moved with sinuous grace where he was, hobbled by the pushed-down jeans. Then Odette changed her position on the sofa so that she could lift her gown. She wanted to spread her legs and masturbate while he danced for her. He lost that dreamy look fast, staring at her.

"Want me to stop?" he asked.

"Not yet." She poured him a stiff drink and handed it to him.

"*Merci, madame,*" he said respectfully. He drank it down all at once, and set the glass on the table, his face a little flushed.

She relaxed with her hand between her legs, watching him cup his heavy balls and start a slow pumping action on his cock again. "Wow. Feeling the rush. How about you?"

"Watching you—yes."

He looked straight into her eyes. "Not much longer. Fuck watching. I want you."

"Ah, Bryan . . ."

"Now?"

"Take them all the way off," she said at last. He did, in less than a second. And then he was over her, sliding his powerful body over the sheer silk of her gown until she slid her fingertip into the ring through his nipple.

That was all it took to control him, strong as he was.

"It hurts," he growled. "Goddamn it—I like it. Keep your finger in the ring."

He kissed her fiercely, fisting his hands in her hair, bruising her lips with passionate tenderness. His overstimulated cock thrust and thrust against her belly, slipping and sliding.

He stopped bucking and forced himself to calm down, looking into her eyes the way he had before, pushing her hair back from her temples. Odette could not quite meet his gaze—the troubled, shadowy quality of it unnerved her.

But that only added to her own arousal. She knew the delicate gown had torn. She didn't care. He could rip it to shreds if he wanted to.

Her hand was pressed between his chest and hers. She couldn't pull out of the little ring that bound them. He had asked her for the pain it gave him as if he wanted to make a sacrifice, however small, for her.

"I wish we could go skin on skin," he said at last. "I know we can't. But I can make it last. I want you to come in my mouth."

He rose up from her body and she eased her fingertip out of the nipple ring. Again he winced. The pressure of his weight had made her finger swell and she had to pull.

"I am sorry." Odette patted his chest, not sure of his mood but loving the wildness that he was trying to control.

"Don't be. That went right to my cock."

So it had. When he stood up, his rod stood nearly upright, longer than before, shiny with more pre-come.

"I should be sorry. I tore your gown."

"I don't care." She took it in her hands and ripped it open down the front, baring herself completely. She seized her breasts, offering them to him as she lay on her back, begging him with her body to lie down with her again.

But he kneeled instead, turning her with her strong hands and pushing her thighs apart.

She moaned when his mouth claimed her pussy and his lascivious tongue penetrated her. Bryan licked and lapped, inside and out, touching her clitoris now and then, but not suckling. She clutched her breasts and squeezed them harder than he would have dared.

His hands slid under her buttocks to clasp and squeeze them, raising her hips so she wouldn't have to, lifting her body to his hungry, loving mouth again and again.

His tongue swirled around her clit when he set her down, but his hands stayed where they were.

It was extremely sensual to have her bottom held by such

big hands. Her softness filled them but his fingers, stretched to their limit, could and did encompass both cheeks of her ass.

Repeatedly, he pushed her buttocks together, then spread them open. Not to look at her asshole, but to excite her by fondling her bottom with firm strength while he ate her pussy.

Odette was lost in the luscious sensation, willing to be as wanton as he desired. Deep inside, she could feel the erotic tension building to the point of no return.

She grabbed his head, straining against his pleasure-giving mouth, shamelessly crying out for more.

Bryan took her clitoris into his mouth and suckled it with little pulses, bringing her to an orgasm so strong that her body lifted up, up, up, taken to a heaven he opened for her alone, where lovemaking was worship . . .

When Odette opened her eyes, Bryan was still kneeling beside her. Wiping his mouth.

"Yeah. Oh yeah. That's what I wanted to happen."

She whimpered her thanks.

"My pleasure. My turn."

Bryan eased what was left of the sheer gown off her, and picked her up. He carried her down the hallway and to her bed. Along the way, held against his chest, Odette found the nipple ring again and slid her finger into it. He only laughed in a low voice and pressed a kiss to her forehead.

She let go of it before he reached the bed and set her down, caressing her and kissing her with abandon.

Odette stroked him wherever she could. "What do you want, my love?" she whispered.

That word. She had said it. Inadvertently. Odette drew in a breath and looked at him. He didn't seem to have heard it. Very well. She still wanted to please him as he had pleased her.

"Those stockings you had on—" He looked around.

"Tie me," she said. "I want to be tied."

He nodded. Instinctively he understood that she needed to cede control to him when all was said and done.

"Where are they?"

"In the bottom of the closet. Or the corner."

Would he tie her ankles or her hands? Or both? Asking would dull the pleasure of giving in to his will. He was naturally gentle despite his considerable strength, he had proved that to her before, during, and after their lovemaking.

She looked at his nakedness as he looked for the stockings. He moved so easily, without a trace of shame or hesitation. Male in every way.

She wanted that huge cock in her pussy, wanted to be completely claimed by him, give herself away . . .

"Here they are." He held up the stockings like a trophy.

Odette shot him a wanton look without saying anything. In her bedroom, he was the boss. She rolled over on her belly, stretching out, facing the headboard.

He didn't waste a minute.

His big hands seized her ankles and dragged her legs far apart.

"Up or down? How do you want me?" she said. Odette didn't turn around.

"Ladies' choice."

She got on all fours and wiggled backward on the bed, presenting her juicy, still swollen labia to him.

"Nice," he growled. "That hot pussy is going to get pounded."

"Mmm." She was waiting for the stockings to be looped around—*whssht*, one ankle was bound to the corner post. *Whssht*—then the other.

She reached out and dragged a pillow toward her. She wanted to hide her face in it, be anonymous, take him deeply and lose herself.

He sat beside her and stroked her back, as if he was gentling a mare he wanted to ride. Odette turned her head, her hair tumbling over her eyes, and looked at him dreamily.

"You are so beautiful," he said. "I feel like I found you this way. Alone. About to pleasure yourself."

She pressed her mouth into the pillow to hide her smile. He was a mind-reader.

"I have tied myself this way," she whispered. "Pretending—pretending that someone would come."

"Really? But you—"

With her head down and her ass up, she was feeling a renewed rush. From the sex, the drinks, and just being alone with him.

"I used a toy. A big rod. Like yours."

He dragged in his breath. "Yeah?"

"In the second drawer," she whispered. "Make me lick it."

She pushed her hair away from her mouth but not her eyes.

Bryan came back and stroked her back again, resting the dildo on the pillow. "Get it wet," he said. He put it to her lips.

Odette opened her mouth and let him guide the dildo inside, tonguing it. She wrapped her lips around it and slicked her toy, naughtily aware that it was making him unbelievably hot to watch her. His body was tense, almost trembling.

"Private pleasure, huh? Women have it made—damn."

She took the dildo out of her mouth, then positioned it just right, holding onto the base as she rose. Her breasts were blush-pink from being squeezed against the bed, and he looked at them avidly.

"But how do you—"

"Practice." Odette eased down on the thick dildo, capturing it in her labia. Then she slid up and down on it, making her tits bounce.

He gasped, watching, grabbing one of her tied ankles. She strained against her bonds, sitting down hard on the bed so the big dildo nearly disappeared.

Odette arched her back and offered Bryan her nipples. Greedily, he sucked one and tugged the other, making it hard for to keep her balance. He seemed to know that and stopped, breathing hard.

She rose to her knees but the dildo stayed in. Halfway in. Sliding out.

Looking to her for a cue, Bryan took it by the base and pushed it gently into her pussy. Not too far.

Odette sighed with satisfaction.

"Ahh," he groaned. "Got it. In and out. Yeah." He pushed and pulled. "Never did this."

"No? But you are skillful. I have never shown that to a boyfriend. You are the only one"—she looked at his huge erection—"who would not be jealous."

"How could I be? Jesus H. Christ, you are so fucking hot, Odette." He eased it out of her. "You're such a lady . . . and such a slut."

"From the back now. In my pussy." She gave a shudder of pleasure and put her face in the pillow. "I can never fuck myself very hard that way. I like to know that you are screwing me with a big dildo and watching. Your eyes—ah, your eyes—" She gave him a last look and put her face in the pillow.

In another moment, he penetrated her again, using gentle but deep thrusts that satisfied her. His passion could be checked by using a dildo on her, but Odette knew that his release would be volcanic from just watching.

The big thick rod, flexible but solid, bobbing inside her pussy—ah, he could feast his eyes on the sight as long as he wanted.

And when he was ready, she would get even more: a real cock, long and hot.

Bryan was ready. He was crazy with lust. There was no aspect of her sexuality that didn't rev him to the max. He took her plaything out of her delectable pussy and put it—oh hell, not back in the drawer, he tossed it on the floor—and went looking for a condom. Sheathed, breaking a sweat, he spread her cheeks and took a horny man's good long look at where he wanted to be.

Rammed all the way up inside the beautiful and way too wanton Odette Gaillard.

He'd tied her loosely enough to move her forward and he simply picked her up around the hips and did it, before she could say yes or no.

He kneeled behind her. Grabbed his cock, slid the head.

Christ, she was tight. And slick.

Whether he'd thrust in or she'd pushed back, he didn't know. But he was in deep. Bryan gave it to her good and hard, not holding back. He grabbed her just above the hips, wild for all of her, craving her goodness and her badness, driving in the prettiest pussy he'd ever seen, satisfying a hunger that was both emotional and physical.

Come . . . was that her telling him to . . . *come!* It was like she was in his mind the second he got into her body and let that mysterious womanliness of hers take him over . . . take him down. He came, shuddering, gasping, almost crying. Trying not to break the soft creature he held. He came hard. So hard.

Like it was the first time.

5

***

The next day . . .

Odette's atelier was a busy place. Bryan couldn't compare it to his mother's little dressmaking shop.

The place reeked of glamour, even though it was clear everyone who worked for her didn't have time for much of it themselves.

He had been introduced to Lucie, dressed in practical black, and flat shoes, and eyed by Marc, in jeans and a T-shirt with *Oh! Oh! Odette* printed on it. He'd shaken hands with her international sales analyst—who looked like every other sales guy Bryan had ever met. Carefully maintained comb-over. Boring white shirt, boring tie.

But then sales analysts weren't paid to be exciting.

All on her own, Odette created the glamour and excitement of her lingerie, and bras and panties.

She'd left him to his own devices for a while, disappearing into a meeting for her next collection.

"Didn't you just do one?" he'd asked.

"Yes. And I must begin the next right away."

"Rush, rush, rush."

"Bryan, if I don't some other designer will knock off my goods and steal my customers."

He got the idea. Fashion was actually not for sissies.

Her staff ignored him politely. She'd told them to. And instructed them not to confiscate his camera if he took pictures, warning him again not to photograph anything that looked like a sketch or a mock-up of an actual design.

There were a few items he did recognize from his mother's shop.

Dressmaker dummies stuck with so many pins they looked like giant voodoo dolls.

Bolts of material, carelessly piled on shelves, as if they were taken out and shoved back a dozen times a day.

Pages torn from magazines and pinned up on bulletin boards.

Buttons, trims, scraps and swatches—all the fribbly stuff he'd played with as a little kid under his mother's sewing table.

It was kind of nice to know that everything wasn't done by computer. But there was no hum of sewing machines in the workshop. Prototypes were made here but that was about it. The staff talked in low voices and several different languages on phones, or typed on computer keyboards.

He took a few shots that didn't break any rules he'd been given, then turned off the little camera to save the battery.

Odette herself would be a lot more interesting to photograph.

Especially her face. Beautiful, sometimes moody, sometimes animated—he loved to look at her.

Too bad they didn't have much more time left.

Fuck whirlwind romance.

He stared out the window, watching pigeons parade on its ledge. A big one—he guessed it was male—was cooing hopefully to a smaller one, probably female. The she-pigeon looked a little doubtful. Double fuck. Was it possible that he sounded just as goofy talking to Odette?

They'd walked over here from her apartment, with her in her apparently favorite place, tucked right under his arm. He'd whispered sweet nothings all the way, interspersed with a few horndog comments that were meant to make her laugh. People had smiled at them. The French really were romantic.

A soft tap on his shoulder turned him around. "Birdwatching?"

"Kinda. Done with the meeting?"

"For now." She took his hand.

"Where are we going?"

"My office."

"Okay." He wasn't all that comfortable with Public Displays of Affection in a workplace, but he kept her hand in his.

He reminded himself that she owned this workplace and could do whatever she wanted. For some reason, that thought didn't ease his mind much.

Odette opened the door, and led him in.

"Wow." Not exactly a sophisticated response, but wow was the word. He'd seen the windows from the outside, been impressed by their height. From the inside, even on an overcast day, it felt like she had the sky for the ceiling. He didn't even look at the rest of the office.

"Like the windows?"

Bryan stopped craning his neck to look at her. "Yeah, I do. Almost feels like being outdoors."

She nodded. "To you most of all. Marc said you were out-doorsy-looking."

"Not exactly," he corrected her. "I like being outdoors. There's a big difference. I'm a California guy. Sun, sand, surf—" He broke off.

Odette was laughing. "You can get the first two in Paris. In summer they pour tons of sand along a part of the Seine. *Voilà!* Instant beach."

He thought of the half-mile long waves at beaches he knew in southern California and the rugged, fogbound beauty of the coastline to the north where he'd done some undergrad research. For a marine biologist, heaven on earth and underwater. Otters, seals, kelp forests—

So go back, he told himself. "That's great," he said. "I'd love to see it. Paris has everything."

"We like to think so. I would like to see California."

"Really? You've never been?"

"*Alors,* no."

"I'm taking you."

She smiled and rubbed her cheek against his shoulder. "Someday soon. For now I am too busy."

"I can see that."

She was different today, all business, from her neat suit she'd worn to impress investors who'd attended the meeting to her severe chignon. He thought the look was interesting; he knew she couldn't always wear funky chic.

But dressed like this, she was a far cry from the wanton woman he'd had so much fun with last night. Was this corporate cutie the real Odette Gaillard?

Hard to tell.

He liked her best of all in black lace. Ripped black lace.

Bryan gave a sigh that made her look up into his face. "What's the matter? Bored or hungry?"

"Neither, babe. Tell me about your new collection."

She smiled and went over to a fat ring binder in the middle of her desk, flipping it open and sticking the sketches under her arm in the middle of the binder.

"I got the idea for it the night I met you at Chez Prune."

He laughed. "It doesn't involve actual prunes, does it?"

"No, no. Prune means plum in French. But no plums either." She looked at him a little wistfully. "It was because it was raining—and I love the rain—"

"It does seem to inspire you." He gave her a wicked grin.

Odette colored slightly. "In many ways, *m'sieu*. Not just sexually."

He held up a hand to indicate that he'd meant no offense. "Sorry. Go on. I'm listening."

"It is the colors. The background of gray intensifies them all. Wet reds. Electric blues. Glowing against black streets. Paris in the rain is beautiful, especially at night . . ." She hesitated, looking anxiously at him. "I was going to you. And that was part of what made it so wonderful."

Bryan just gaped at her. What in the hell could he say? She had just about made up a love poem on the spot. He couldn't top that, not in a million years.

"I think I understand," he said finally.

The anxious look had disappeared from her face when he looked at her again.

"Anyway, I had been playing with this unusual gray silk—" All business, she pulled out a swatch from somewhere in the ring binder and waved it at him. "It shimmers beautifully. And the phrase *Paris in the rain* seemed to go with it. I thought it might do for a design concept."

"Did your, uh, team like it?"

"No," she said crossly. "Not any more than you seem to. I suppose it is too personal."

He studied her for a long moment, still unsure of what to say.

"Fashion has to appeal to many, many people to be profitable. So it is not all about, tra la, my incredible creativity."

"You are really creative. And a really good businesswoman." The words sounded a little forced, but he did mean them.

Odette sniffed. "I should make up my mind and be one or the other."

"Do you have to?"

"No." She shut the ring binder and sat down in her swivel chair. "Not yet. I need to grow the brand for a few more years, license the name—then I can get out."

"You want to?"

"I don't want to hate what I do. Eventually some gigantic corporation will gobble me up. Even if they don't, I have enough money to live on for the rest of my life right now."

"Congratulations. Wish I could say that."

Odette put her arms on the arms of the chair, and rocked. "I have been very lucky."

"I think there's more to it than that."

"I know what women like. And I know how to design fashion that is inexpensive to make, but can be sold for a fortune. Josi Natori did the same thing with little silky robes. I didn't invent the business model either."

"Okay, okay." He was baffled by her bad mood. "I don't really know what I'm talking about, so I should probably shut up."

"You are being nice to me." She glowered at him.

Bryan blew out an exasperated breath. "I will never understand why women get pissed off about that."

"Because you don't take us seriously."

"Odette, please. We don't have a whole lot of hours left. Could you save this for the next—"

"For the next guy? Is that what you were going to say?"

"No." He was pissed off now. Just a little. But definitely pissed off. "I was going to say the next time we met. I was thinking of coming back."

"You were?"

"Yeah. Unless you don't want me to."

Odette shook her head. "I do. I am sorry, Bryan. The meeting did not go well and I am taking it out on you."

"Don't sweat it."

She began to pace and he noticed the track in the carpet. Apparently she did it a lot.

"Ruffles and bows. Sugar and spice. Little mice with big eyes—*mon Dieu!*" She threw up her hands. "The Japanese are my biggest customers right now and they want cuteness—they call it *kawaii*. So I will learn to be cute," she hissed.

He had to smile. His beautiful she-cat looked like she could eat cute little mice for breakfast, lunch, and dinner right now.

"It's not the end of the world," he said gently. She was entitled to be temperamental. Even his mom had grumbled about adding Cinderella bows to the backs of prom gowns and wedding dresses. Like a neon sign for Look At My Big Butt, she'd said.

"No. I suppose not. Thank you for listening."

"No problem."

She went back to her desk and checked her planner next. "The fitting models are coming in soon. Do you want to watch that?"

"Am I allowed to?"

"Of course."

"Anything I need to know first?"

"They stand around with no clothes on. We have to turn the heat up."

He gave her a wry smile. "Sure. I'll watch."

Odette with pins in her mouth and a measuring tape around her neck and glasses sliding down her nose was yet another different woman.

He could tell she liked working with her hands. The experience transformed her.

He tried not to stare at the naked fitting model, but Grischenka Oblomov didn't seem to care. She looked off into space, over his head. Close up, models just weren't that great as far he was concerned.

Okay, on the plus side, this one had ruler-straight, white-blond hair down to her waist and apple boobs. But she was six and a half feet tall, with skeletal legs and no ass. Both minuses.

Odette had caught him scoping Grischenka out before they reached the glassed-in fitting room. "She has perfect breasts. That's all I need to fit a bra design. Everything below that is of no consequence."

"Got it."

He didn't like himself for judging the model the way he had, even if Grischenka did seem kind of d-u-m-b. But she obviously hadn't eaten for days and she couldn't help the body she'd been born with.

Judgy-Wudgy was a bear, he told himself. Was the fashion mindset catching?

He looked over Odette's shoulder into the mirror and wondered what the hell she saw in him.

It was the second time around for the wool sweater he'd worn to Chez Prune and it still wasn't quite dry. He pushed up

the sleeves. The damp cuffs were irritating. Then he ran a hand
through hair he didn't even look at as a rule, trying to shape it a
little.

Marc came in waving a sketch and Odette *p'too*-ed the pins
out of her mouth and put them in her pocket. He conferred in
French with her, then went out again, giving Bryan a brief
wave. He'd handed Odette the sketch—she was frowning at it
now while Grischenka stood and yawned, then looked at her
nails which were bitten down to the quick.

Bryan corrected himself. She had eaten.

She wasn't completely naked. A tiny, tiny thong covered her
pubes. He didn't feel a flicker of interest. Grischenka was twitchy
and vacant, and Odette had probably ruined him for any other
woman.

What a woman she was.

"Flower petals," she was saying. "That I can do myself.
Lucie!" She went to the door and called for her assistant.

"I'm right here. You don't have to yell."

"I didn't see you."

"What do you need?"

Lucie seemed well-trained in fetching. Bryan folded his
arms and waited on the sidelines.

"The styling wand and some pink silk scraps, please."

Her assistant nodded and went to get both.

"I am going to play God and make flowers," Odette said. She
slid a tape measure around the fitting model's waist. "Grischenka,
stand still. Can you do that?"

"*Da.*"

"Thank you."

She lifted the tape to the model's nipples and Grischenka
trembled. That got to Bryan. Not now, Wonder Dick, he said
silently. Go back in the Dick Cave.

Odette had given him another prototype pair of briefs, but these were a little too big. She seemed to think nothing of handling another woman's breasts, but he was definitely going to have to adjust his junk or tie the baggy briefs in a no-nonsense knot if he had to watch her do it much longer.

Bryan looked at the ceiling.

Odette had removed the tape and was making notes on the sketch when he looked down again. Grischenka's nipples were red where the tape had been.

Bryan decided to study the floor.

"Here you are," Lucie said. "What's the matter with him?"

He was the only him, so Bryan assumed that Lucie's assistant was looking at him.

"Hot in here," Odette said absently. "Thank you, Lucie. This will do nicely."

He heard the snipping of scissors and took a deep breath. Then he looked steadily and exclusively at Odette. She was cutting circles and ovals out of the pink silk that Lucie had brought.

Then she set them on a table and shook up an aerosol can, spraying them lightly with some kind of starch or stiffener. Whatever it was, it made him a little light-headed. No one else seemed to mind it.

Odette jammed the styling wand plug into a wall outlet and let it heat up, putting her hands on her hips and smiling at Bryan. He cheered up. Maybe they could get in a four o'clock.

No, Parisians ate late. Six o'clock would be even better for sex.

She checked the temperature of the wand by holding it near her hand, then took one of the damp ovals and formed it into a petal. She did all the others quickly after that, setting them down one by one.

Grischenka's arms were folded over her pretty breasts. Bryan hoped the petals would end up there.

Sure enough. Hell fucking yes. Odette picked up a stiffened petal and rested it lightly on the model's nipple.

Shoot . . . me . . . now. Bryan hoped he looked bored, instead of like a slavering, sex-crazed dog to end all dogs. He checked. His long, lascivious tongue was behind his teeth.

Was Odette torturing him on purpose? He had to sit down and cross his legs. The semen was five feet high and rising.

Problem: there was no chair.

Solution: suffer.

Odette placed a second petal on the model's other nipple.

"Grischenka, don't breathe," she said laughingly.

"*Da.*"

The one word made the petal flutter off, and Odette gently turned the model's head to one side. "Breathe away from them."

Something about the way she held the other woman's chin made Bryan think of girl-on-girl porno. Chicks kissing. Yeah.

She put the fallen petal back, not even looking at Bryan. Then, using bits of bodystick tape, she attached all the rest, barely covering Grischenka's perfect breasts.

"There," she said to Bryan, standing back to study the effect. "I want it to look like the petals just fell there."

"I think you succeeded." He was glad to have something to say, and grateful he had a legitimate reason to look at Grischenka's breasts.

He hadn't known it was possible to like only one part of a woman, but he did now, because Grischenka wasn't interesting in any other way.

The way Odette handled her was *very* interesting.

"I prefer to design directly on the body," she was saying. "The result is body-conscious, you see."

"Yes." He nodded. Slavering dog.

"I might try panties to match," she mused. She pulled on the threadlike elastic that held Grischenka's thong in place. Almost against his will, Bryan glanced down at her pubes and saw a completely shaved slit.

Odette better not touch that. He'd fucking vaporize on the spot.

She took the biggest petal and folded one edge over the top of the tiny front panel of the thong. Touching that.

Bryan wanted to whip off his wool sweater and jump on it the way Tom Cruise had jumped on Oprah's couch. Making a point. Joy to the world. Let's go crazy.

Something like that.

"Mind if I go out for a cup of coffee?" he asked Odette.

"There is excellent coffee in the break room. Tell Delphine I want one too. She knows how I like it."

"Be right back. Grischenka, anything for you?"

The model gave him an appalled look and shook her head. "*Nyet.*"

Delphine turned out to be a doe-eyed beauty from the Riviera who was working her way through fashion school by serving coffee to the staff of Odette's atelier.

They talked surfing for a little while—apparently, the Mediterranean produced waves at least fifteen inches high, who knew—and he took the coffees back to the fitting room.

Grischenka's ass was fluttering. Flat to begin with, it looked good now.

"Pretty, no?" Odette asked him.

"Very nice." He kept holding the coffees. "Here ya go."

"*Merci.*" Odette took the cup marked with an O and set it down, prying off the lid to let it cool. "Thank you, Bryan."

Grischenka was squinting at the clock on the wall.

"Oh, do you have to go? I'll take these off you. But let me photograph you first—Bryan, do you still have that camera?"

Did he want Grischenka's fluttering ass on his memory chip? Sweet dreams were made of this. "Sure," he said. "In my pocket. Hang on." He set down his cup of coffee and retrieved it for her.

Like a robot, the fitting model turned around step by step, letting Odette snap photo after photo. She handed the camera back to Bryan.

"Thanks."

Then she kneeled in front the model and pulled her flower-petal panties down. Slowly. Not a petal came loose.

He *still* wasn't turned on by Grischenka, but Odette's action had opened the floodgates of fantasy. Bryan picked up his coffee and stared into it so hard the breath from his nostrils made ripples in it.

Odette rose and plucked the petals from Grischenka's breasts, then picked off the bodystick tape. The model thanked her, and went over to a bulging bag, pulling out a sweater and jeans, which she put on as casually as if she'd been in a women's locker room.

Odette thanked her and Grischenka left.

Bryan took a nonchalant sip of his coffee. "What now?"

"Men's underwear," Odette said sweetly.

"Whew. That I can handle."

She burst out laughing. "It wasn't very nice of me to turn a girl into a flower in front of you."

"I honestly didn't mind," he said, "but for a while there, I was headed for meltdown."

"But you didn't." Her eyes danced with amusement. "You are stronger than you know, Bryan."

"Thanks. Just remember, you're the one I want."

"Is that so?"

He put down his coffee, pulled her into his arms, and kissed her breathless.

"Mrmf," she said, squirming away. "I have to get back to work."

"Bring on the dude."

Lucie escorted the next model in after a few minutes. He was tall, with a swimmer's body, and had a nicer ass than lanky Grischenka.

At least Odette seemed to think so. She kept looking at it. He wore a man-thong-thing that looked weird. Studying flawless male butts couldn't be entirely work for her, Bryan thought sourly.

"Turn around, please, Johan."

He obeyed, hands on hips.

"Pose."

He struck various attitudes. Nothing ridiculous like a bodybuilder, but Bryan still felt annoyed.

Odette was now studying his package.

Mr. Big Stuff had won the genetic lottery in that department. Bryan felt outdone. Of course, the really super-extra-longs didn't always get longer when excited, or so a couple of girlfriends had told him.

What did Bryan know? He had a degree in marine biology, not human anatomy. But he was pretty sure only a male whale could beat Johan.

Odette whipped out the tape. Same routine. Around the waist. Around the nipples. She might as well have been measuring a cast-iron streetlamp for all that Johan reacted.

He just stood there, blinking.

Then Odette kneeled in front of him.

Was she going to measure the guy's inseam? Or his—no. Bryan was heading out if she did.

"You hold that end there," she instructed him, pointing to where his thighs joined the army.

He relaxed a little. She wasn't going in. Johan would have to touch his own nuts to get measured.

She got a measurement to the knee, then held up a piece of soft dark cotton, spreading it over Johan's quad.

"Nice and stretchy," she said approvingly. "This might work. Lucie—"

The assistant had never gone away, Bryan realized.

"Hold that there for me." Odette got up and went to get a few pins.

Lucie kneeled and looked up at Johan adoringly. He gave her a slight smile.

Johan, if you like girls, you have a date, he thought. Bryan couldn't really read the guy. Maybe his jealousy was getting to him.

Odette came back and kneeled next to Lucie. Both of them giggled.

He was definitely jealous.

"Lucie, you slide a finger under there and I'll pin this on. Johan, don't move."

"*Ja.*"

"I'm thinking of men's swim trunks, circa 1925," she explained, looking up at Bryan. "Worn tight. With a striped tank. Very sexy look."

He only nodded.

She took a pin, placed it and—Johan moved.

"*Ach! Bitte, nein!*"

Was that German for *don't castrate me*? Bryan thought so.

"I am so sorry, Johan," Odette said, flustered. "Lucie, you do it."

Her assistant pinned the material where her boss had tried to. She managed not to stick Johan, who relaxed visibly.

The rest of the fitting went quickly. Nothing about it interested Bryan, who was glad when it was over.

"So," she said when they were back in her office. "Now you have an idea of what I do all day."

That, and an idea that seeing her with another woman turned him on, but he suspected she was too fiery and jealous to tolerate a threesome, let alone enjoy it. No biggie. He'd done it once with someone else and her girlfriend, hadn't been a life-changing experience.

Bryan understood wanting to have your lover all to yourself. He'd gotten an even clearer idea that seeing her with another man made him want to punch something like a wall. Or the man.

"Also you have a few pictures for your mother," she was saying.

"None of you."

Odette frowned. "Why would you send a picture of me to her?"

"Okay, it's not for her. I mean, she would be curious but she can look you up online."

"Pah. Meaningless, all that."

He gave her a surprised look. "You're a big goddamn deal whether you think it's meaningless or not. Do you know how many hits came up for your name? About fifteen thousand. Your designs and your shows, more than fifty thousand."

"Lucie handles publicity for me. I have never looked. What of it?"

"You're famous, Odette."

"I know that. But I am not recognized on the street as a rule and I don't care. Do you?"

He was quiet for a little while, thinking it over. "No. not really. But—"

"But what?" she asked defensively. "Are we so very different?"

"Well, yeah. Hell, yeah. I'm nobody."

"Not to me."

He studied her face. Her beautiful, changeable, moody, one-of-a-kind face. All he wanted right now was one good photograph of her so he could look at it back in California and remind himself that this three-day dream had actually happened when it was over.

"If you want my picture, then take it," she said. "So long as I can take one of you."

Without asking her to smile, he lifted the camera and looked into the viewscreen. Her eyes were compelling enough to belong to a movie actress from long ago, her lips sensually full. She did remind him of a famous French actress, but which one?

He tried to recall the hours he'd spent slumped in the UCSC campus theater, watching classic movies for a buck. Someone from a while ago. Not Catherine Deneuve. Too perfect. No, the other one, the actress with the world-weary beauty that shone with intelligence. She'd been in a great black-and-white movie he'd rented from Netflix. *Jules et Jim.* Yeah. Jeanne Moreau. Odette looked a lot like her.

He pressed the shutter button and looked up at the real woman. Odette Gaillard was impossible to capture.

"Happy now?" she asked.

"You don't seem to be. Sorry if you don't like having your picture taken. I wanted one that wasn't official. You as you are."

"Hmm. But that is why I brought you here to my atelier.

Yes, yes"—she waved away the words that weren't quite out of his mouth—"you wanted to tour the place to get a few souvenir pictures for your *maman* and I didn't mind—oh, Bryan. She must be a very nice lady to have raised a son like you and all by herself too."

"I'll tell her you said so. She won't believe me. Let's get back to what you were saying before that. I think I missed something important."

Odette stared down at the bulging ring binder that held too much.

"I wanted to show you that I worked for a living. That I am not a stupid slave to fashion—it just happens to be what I do."

"I'm not following you."

"I don't know how to say this without sounding like a fool."

He gave her a level look, but he was hella curious. "Just say it."

"I was—because I am—in love with you. I think."

Bryan sucked in a sharp breath. "You think?"

"I have never been in love before. In lust, yes," she said honestly. "And I am in lust with you too."

"Good."

"So what do you think?" she asked him. "I expect complete honesty. Nothing less."

"About you loving me?"

"Yes." She smiled slowly. "It sounds nice when you say it."

"I—I'm honored. But also freaked out."

"Why?"

"Women like you don't fall in love with guys like me. And—and I can't say I'm *completely* sure I love you."

She gave a very Gallic shrug. "*Tant pis*, eh? That's how it goes. Oh, well. You leave tomorrow."

He could see tears shimmering in her eyes.

"But I'm ninety percent sure I do. Love you, I mean."

"You are?"

"And I'm absolutely positive I'm in lust with you, Odette. The lust is no problem at all for me."

She fell silent. "Hmm. It could work."

"Not if I'm leaving tomorrow."

6

Lucie chose that moment to burst in. "Odette! The worst has happened! You must come quickly!"

Go fuck Johan, Bryan thought angrily.

"What is it, Lucie? Is the building on fire?" She got up quickly and went to her assistant.

"No, of course not!" Lucie didn't even seem to notice that Bryan was in the room. "Come look on my computer! *Merde!* I am so angry!"

Bryan looked around the office. He hadn't even realized until then that Odette had no computer on her desk or anywhere. No laptop, either. She really was a hands-on designer.

Odette let Lucie drag her away, casting an alarmed look over her shoulder at Bryan.

Should he stay here or wait for the women to come back? He settled down for what he hoped would be a short wait. Something major must have happened. Lucie wasn't the excitable type.

Half an hour later, they hadn't returned. He stood, and went out, heading for Lucie's office. It had to be her office, there were a lot of people clustered around the door and probably more inside, chattering angrily.

He translated a few key phrases in his mind. *Copies made. For sale now. The new line is not out yet. There are not even prototypes.*

Bryan could see over the heads of the small crowd. Odette was in Lucie's office, her face illuminated by the faint bluish light coming from the screen.

She glanced up briefly at Bryan, then issued instructions in a rapid-fire, low voice to key members of her staff. She shooed the others away.

He didn't know whether to stay or go. Whatever had happened, it was serious. Odette looked down at the laptop again, hit a few keys, then motioned him over.

"My latest designs have been copied."

"The ones from the runway show? That was less than two days ago."

"Not those. Already old news. No, the very latest." She pointed to the screen. "Look."

He leaned in and saw flower-petal undies and a bra on a white plastic dummy with no head, no arms, and no legs.

"You just did those!"

"Yes, I know," she said acidly. "And that's not all." She clicked on several thumbnails. Designs he hadn't seen, just as imaginative, bloomed and faded away.

"That can't be. You created that design right on Grischenka." He stopped for a second. "Wait a minute. Could she—"

"I had sketched them before I worked with the actual materials. But I keep things like that in my binder."

"Not on a computer?"

"Not until the final stages of design, no. We've been hacked before."

Bryan shook his head. "So what happens now?"

"We go after these thieves. File suit for trademark infringement."

He nodded, and then something else occurred to him. "But don't fashions get copied all the time?"

"Yes," she said. Exasperation tightened her features. "There actually isn't that much we can ultimately do. But these designs were meant for my Japanese clients. If they aren't assured of an exclusive line, they won't buy."

He was getting an idea of why Lucie said the worst had happened. "How much money is involved?"

"Millions."

"If you can't stop this, will the company go under?"

"No. But my credibility as a designer who can deliver is going to be very shaky, though."

"But you own the company, right? So it's not like you're going to get fired and replaced."

Odette shook her head and pressed her lips together, fighting back emotions. He knew her well enough by now to read them.

Fury. Helplessness. Sorrow.

Hell, she was up against it. And there was nothing he could do to help her.

"If our earnings drop too low, I might have to sell. And Oh! Oh! Odette could be the object of a hostile takeover. And then, yes—I could be fired."

What she was saying was unthinkable. But Bryan knew it could happen.

"Let's think this through." He looked around at the other people in the room, who'd been listening to Odette with solemn expressions. "Just you and me."

"You have no expertise in this, Bryan." She chewed her bottom lip.

"Maybe that's good," he said. "As an outsider . . ."

She glanced up at him, understanding what he didn't want to say. As an outsider, he couldn't possibly be the culprit. Anyone, including the onlookers, who worked for her, could be the one who'd sold her out.

"All right. Gaston, Cherie, will you download these and call the legal department?" A man and a woman stepped forward, but Lucie didn't move away from her desk.

"I'll send the link to you and to legal," Lucie said. "Odette, what do you want me to do?"

"Just monitor the site for now. Note the keywords and check them on Google at least once an hour. The designs are probably all over the world by now."

"What does that mean?"

"That they are worthless, at least to me. Whoever is manufacturing them will get them into stores in countries with no meaningful trademark protection. With my name on the label."

"Panty pirates," Bryan said without thinking.

Odette slapped him. "That's not funny!"

Bryan put a hand to his stinging cheek. "Sorry. Jesus, I really am."

She stormed out of the room and he went after her. "Odette, please—"

The low walls of the cubicles and workstations made it easy to follow her, even though she was moving fast.

He nodded to the employees who stood up, looking after her curiously and looking at him with narrowed eyes.

If nothing else, most of her staff was loyal to her, Bryan thought. He didn't want to run. They'd probably call security and he'd get the bum's rush to the sidewalk outside the atelier. He heard a door bang in the corridor ahead.

He smiled politely as he walked a little faster. When he got to her office door, it was shut.

Not quite, he saw on a second look. She'd banged it so hard, the latch had let go. He put a hand on it and eased it open a little. Christ. If he poked his head in, she might throw something heavy at him.

"Mind if I come in?" he said from the other side.

He heard an angry sob being swallowed back and then a somewhat more controlled, "No."

"I really am sorry, Odette."

"So am I. It's not your fault, what happened. I lost my temper in front of my staff—I didn't want to do that."

"Can't be the first time."

She looked at him indignantly. "How would you know?"

"Designer temperament. You have it."

She folded her arms over her chest. "You happen to be right, but I am the CEO. It's one thing to lose your temper over creative problems, but not something like this."

"What do you mean?"

"Those people depend on me. I pay their salaries. Someone is in charge around here and it happens to be me."

"I'm sure they understand," he said soothingly.

"Maybe." Her voice was dull. She looked up at the clouds passing over her skyhigh windows. "What am I going to do?"

"Calm down, first of all. Deep breaths."

She tried one, and started to cough.

"Again. C'mon."

"Fuck off, Bryan!"

"No. You have to get a grip. Forgive me for getting all California on you, but deep breathing does help."

"What's next?" she snarled. "Sitting in the lotus position? Will that help?"

"Okay, okay." He held up in his hands. "Time out. You can calm down later. Maybe frantic is the way to go right now."

"Arggghhh!" With a cry of despair, she put her hands over her face.

Well, he could stay calm and let her vent for a while. She didn't make any more anguished noises and she was breathing a little more slowly. Through her fingers.

"Has this ever happened before?"

"Once. When I first started. But the label was new and not worth copying. We got a cease-and-desist order through our contact at the Ministry of Trade and that was the end of it."

"So now what?"

She rubbed her eyes. "I suck it up, as you Americans say. And hire a detective to find the culprit."

"Wouldn't you rather investigate in-house?"

Odette snorted. "I don't have anyone on staff like that. No, someone from outside would be better. There are specialists, although I am sure they are incredibly expensive."

"Cheaper than the company going under."

"Would you please not point out the obvious?" she asked with a pained expression. "Even if it is true."

"Sorry."

"I will make some calls and find out who takes cases like these. Paris is still the design capital of the world. I am sure it is a lucrative specialty."

She unzipped her purse, looking in an inside pocket for something, and came up with keys. Then she unlocked a drawer in her desk and pulled out a laptop.

"You do have one. I thought it was kind of weird that you didn't—"

She'd opened it before he finished the sentence. "Of course I do," she said, booting it up. She stared into the screen, but he had the feeling she was aware of every move he made and every breath he took at this charged moment. "Not on the company network and encrypted up the kazoo. What is a kazoo, by the way?"

"A musical instrument for kids. It honks. And it's a nasty metaphor for—"

"I get the idea. Another wonderful American expression."

"Whoa," he said. "Are you in an anti-U.S. mood all of a sudden? Yankee Go Home and all that?"

"No. I am just being a bitch and taking it out on you."

That stopped him. "Thanks for being honest," he said dryly.

"I want you to stay longer," she said, still not looking at him. "You can't leave tomorrow. I need you here."

"Odette, I don't know the first thing about—corporate espionage or trademark infringement or anything like that."

"I need you," she repeated vehemently.

"I'll see what I can do," he said. He wasn't sure if he had enough money in his account to cover a ticket change and he was damned if he'd ask her. Even if she offered, he wouldn't accept.

Being footloose and fancy-free was just another way of saying you were fucked in the money department.

Bryan looked around her spare office, thinking that few pieces of furniture in it probably cost around what he made in a year taking assistant gigs in the biology department.

The university parceled out the jobs to broke grad students like him, but that didn't mean he could cover his expenses or had an emergency fund.

Did her problems qualify as an emergency? Hell, yes. But she was the one with the deep pockets, not him.

More than anything, he wanted to be her knight in shining armor. It was too damn bad he didn't have a bag of golden ducats hanging off his freaking chain mail. When you wanted to man up, and didn't have the money to do it, life sucked.

"Okay. I'm going to leave for a bit," he said. "Try not to jump out the window, okay?"

She was clicking away on the laptop, but she looked up. "Are you coming back? Are you staying?"

"Yes. And yes, I think so. I want to take care of that first. You know how it is with last-minute ticket changes."

"Do you need money?"

"No."

Just that she'd asked that question rankled him. Bryan walked through the streets of the neighborhood around her atelier, looking for a cheap place to eat.

The internet café he'd stopped into before didn't serve sandwiches, so that was out. He needed protein before he tackled the airline reservation problem. As in round, ground cow slathered in ketchup, topped and bottomed with a toasted bun.

Where was the diner he'd been to with her?

Somewhere east of the river and west of his hotel. Meaning he had no idea. And speaking of the hotel, he was going to have to check out of it.

They could hold his duffel and backpack hostage if they wanted to. He hadn't brought a laptop or anything of value. Bryan was a big believer in traveling light.

He'd blown it. Getting involved with a woman like Odette Gaillard meant *beaucoup de* emotional baggage he wasn't sure he wanted to claim.

The sound of running feet behind him made him turn his head to get out of the jogger's way. But it wasn't a jogger. It was Marc, Odette's male assistant.

"You walk fast," Marc panted.

"Yeah, I do. You all right? I didn't know you were trying to catch up with me."

The other man took huge, gulping breaths. "I detest exercise."

Marc didn't look like he needed it. He was lithe and lean, but he was completely out of breath. "Sorry," Bryan said.

Marc took a pack of Gauloises out of his pants pocket and fired one up. "Do you mind?"

"Nah. Smoke one for me."

The assistant grinned, holding the end of his cigarette in his teeth, squinting his eyes against the smoke. "Do you believe we French are no longer allowed to smoke wherever we want?" He held the end near his lips with his fingertips and took a deep drag. "First they banned smoking in restaurants and now bars and cafés. It is an outrage."

"It's the way the world is going."

"Pah. Me, I believe in *liberté*, *égalité*, and tobacco."

"Whatever floats your boat, Marc. So why were you chasing after me?"

The other man eyed a guy who looked just like him, only Latin, and didn't respond for a second. "My apologies. What a distraction." He coughed and waved the cigarette he'd taken out of his mouth, making Bryan cough too.

"It's okay."

"I wanted to make sure," Marc began again, "that you were not going to disappear. Odette is crushed on you."

"Do you mean she has a crush on me or that she is crushed by me?"

"English is a stupid language," he sighed. "I mean that she thinks you are hot."

"The first, then."

Marc threw his half-smoked cigarette into the gutter. "She is not wrong. But I suspect that—ah—perhaps the subject is a delicate one."

"Spit it out," Bryan said, not delicately.

"You don't have a dime. Is that the right word? Dimes are the little coins, yes?"

Bryan thrust his hands in his pockets and walked a little faster. He was, in fact, dimeless. "Uh-huh. Easy to lose."

"I thought so."

Bryan shot him a look. "Do I look poor to you? I mean, most Americans wear jeans and tops. So do a lot of the French."

"Do not get pissy with me," Marc said severely. "No, it is not your clothes. You have a ragged charm that is interesting."

Holy fuck. Never in his life had Bryan heard a line like that. He had to laugh a little. "Thanks."

"It is the look in your eyes. That is how I know."

Marc wasn't wrong about him having no money, so Bryan wasn't going to argue. "Whatever," he said resignedly. "You're right, I am pretty much broke. I can't tell Odette that."

"I understand. A man must be a man. But Odette needs you. When you left the atelier, she burst into tears and cried like a baby."

"Oh." Bryan gave a huge sigh and stopped. "Can we sit here by the *quai* and talk about this?"

"Of course." Marc led the way to the stone wall and jumped down. A group of old fishermen with massive backs and flat caps sat with lines in the water, not speaking. They looked almost like statues, but trails of smoke wafted upward from the cigars wedged in the corners of their mouths.

"Catch anything?" Bryan asked.

One of the men grunted and shifted his stumpy cigar to the other side. "*Rien. Tant pis.*"

"Nothing. Tough luck. Right." If he didn't figure out his money problems, he could join these guys. Mark looked at the silvery-gray river, running on to the next bridge. The Seine had a lot of them.

He sat next to Marc on a low, projecting wall some distance away from the fishermen, and gave him a rueful smile. "Look, I want to help her, I really do. But I have to have a place to stay, and I'm going to need to hit up a friend in the states for a loan to stay longer."

"Wire transfer," Marc said immediately.

"What, did you figure all this out while you were running after me?"

"*Oui.*"

Bryan shot him a sideways look. "You really care about Odette, don't you?"

"She is the best. She is good to her staff. But if she has the stress, we all have the stress."

He nodded. "I can believe it. Nice of you to look after her, dude."

Marc gave a shrug and looked out at the river. "She would be angry if she knew I asked you this."

"I can keep my mouth shut."

"Good. Please do. As to the question of where you can stay, the answer is with me. I have a convertible couch where you can sleep, and my boyfriend is a chef who brings home disgustingly rich food. You will be doing us a favor by eating it. And we have a Chihuahua if you get lonely. We don't get home until three in the morning, so you will have the place to yourself most of the time. Do you like dogs?"

Sure, Bryan wanted to say, *except for the ones that fit on a Ritz cracker*. But he couldn't turn down free room and board. "Love 'em. I'll walk the little guy for you."

"He walks inside my shoulder bag. Not on the street."

"Nothing doing. I draw the line there, Marc," Bryan laughed. "Paws on the pavement. A dog must be a dog."

Marc grinned and shook another Gauloise out of the pack. He cupped his hands around the end and lit it, squinting at Marc through the smoke. "It is a deal. Settle your bill at the hotel and take a taxi over. We live in the Marais."

"Is that in Paris?"

"*Bien sûr.*"

7

Good enough. He'd lugged his stuff over to Marc and Achille's apartment in the Marais. It looked like an interesting neighborhood, with old buildings and a variety of people.

Okay, a lot seemed to assume that he, Bryan, was gay, but since they didn't seem to care one way or the other, he decided that he didn't either.

Their apartment was spacious, with eccentric décor that looked like odd wayfarers had put their feet up on it. He'd stashed his stuff in a gigantic Moroccan trunk and been solemnly introduced to a tiny Chihuahua named Jimmy which trembled when he patted it, then licked his hand. The dog stayed on the floor, studying him with bulging eyes.

"You see, he approves," Marc said. He scooped the dog and handed it to Achille, a very tall, brawny man whose huge hands almost engulfed it.

Marc's boyfriend nodded. "We only let people stay if Jimmy likes them." He rubbed the dog's head affectionately and the Chihuahua closed its eyes and panted.

"Where are you going?" Marc asked him.

"To the Boulevard des Batignolles for squash blossoms and whatever else catches my fancy." Achille put the dog in one of the cavernous pockets of his canvas jacket and Jimmy settled down as if he were used to traveling there.

"I'll come with you. Do you want to go, Bryan?" Marc asked. "It is an organic farmer's market. Very good produce."

"Ah—" he hesitated. "I was thinking of heading over to Odette's. I could give her a bunch of carrots but I don't think she'd be too thrilled."

"No, she wouldn't," Marc laughed. "*Bien.* There are towels in the cupboard in the bathroom. Help yourself to whatever you need and do whatever you want and we will see you when we see you."

"Thanks, guys."

Achille stuffed several string bags in his other pocket and the two men left, calling out good-byes as they went down the stairs.

He'd gotten cleaned up and shaved, then unfolded a map to figure out how to get back to Odette's.

It was past seven, she ought to be home by now. He'd tried her cell, nothing doing there, and left a message. There was no answer at her office number.

Bryan didn't feel like sitting here or wandering around his new neighborhood when he knew she had to be overwhelmed. He would just get there, because it would take a while, then call her again.

It took longer than he thought. He wasn't on her street until after nine. Negotiating a big, unfamiliar city was kind of a pain until you got the lay of the land, and Paris was a mix of straight, wide boulevards that went on forever, and crooked little streets that doubled back on themselves.

Anyway, he made it.

Bryan stood on the cobblestones outside her building and punched in her number. It rang as he looked up at her windows,

130

hoping to see a glimpse of her in her apartment. He thought he did but he couldn't be sure. Very faintly, he heard her phone ring and then stop.

Huh. The lights were on.

He tried the number again and this time she answered.

"Hello, Bryan." Her voice sounded weary.

"Oh—yes, it's me." Why was he surprised that the French had caller ID? Her neighborhood was so old-fashioned that it seemed out of place. "Um, how are you doing?"

"I have found out nothing."

"Want to talk about it?"

She sighed heavily. "Where are you?"

"On the street where you live." Should he burst into the song and get all romantic? Nah. It probably wouldn't make her smile, let alone laugh.

"Okay. Then come up."

"You sure? Maybe you're not in the mood for company." He heard a tapping and looked up.

She was at her window, phone to her ear, gazing down at him. Her mouth was turned down in a sad frown and her hair was pinned up. Around her body was a towel that didn't conceal all of her, but it was trying.

"I was about to take a bath," she said.

"Aha. Want your back washed?"

He saw her dash away tears with the hand that wasn't holding the phone.

"Yes. I do."

"Be right there." He clicked the phone shut, slipped it into his jacket pocket, and made his move. Buzzed through the door, he ran up the stairs to her apartment, taking her in his arms the second he stepped in.

She was struggling to hang on to her towel, hug him back, and rub at her swollen eyes. The towel lost.

Bryan didn't have a problem with that.

But he wasn't going to use her misery as an excuse to jump her. No, he would rot in the hell reserved for Men Who Just Didn't Care About Anyone But Themselves if he did that.

He would wash her back. Rub her feet. Wipe away her tears. Soothe her. Comfort her.

Then he would jump her. If she wanted him to.

There were trails of fragrant steam issuing from the bathroom, and she padded that way. He actually had never seen her just walking around in an everyday way. She looked fantastic.

Her beautifully shaped, strong legs weren't the only beneficiaries of her jump-for-joy lifestyle. Her butt, from the back, was just as toned and amazingly curvy too.

Do not grab, he told himself. He followed, waiting for the moment when she would turn around and kiss him again.

But she didn't, because she was sniffling and too proud to cry in front of him for long. He kept a respectful distance, even though it killed him. Odette stopped by the tub and bent down to test the water temperature with her hand.

"Smells good," he said. "What is that?"

"Lavender essence from Provence. I was hoping to go there in June. But now, with this business of the theft, I will not."

"Is it that bad, Odette?"

She flicked the water off her fingertips and absentmindedly took the hand he proffered to climb into her bath.

"I spoke to an investigator today. He says it will take months to resolve."

"Why?" He watched one of her feet touch the bottom of the bath through the clear water, and then the other. She stood there unself-consciously, curling her toes as she bent down to splash lavender-scented water on her thighs. She was like a goddamn nymph. A nymph with a multimillion-dollar business empire to run.

"There is no telling where the designs and whoever paid to have them stolen will turn up. He will begin in Paris, but he is sure they have gone halfway around the world. He wants to fly to Asia and work his way through all those countries—ahhh."

She squatted down in the water and her ass cheeks parted as she balanced on her heels. Then she got on all fours, about to turn over and loll in the enormous bathtub.

Bryan swallowed hard when Odette looked up at him. Her pinned-up hair had a few tendrils coming down, curling over her shoulders and down the nape of her neck. "Do we have to talk about it now?"

"No. Hell, no."

"Good." She went down into the water, and did a tuck and roll that gave him a glimpse of pink pussy, then sat with her knees folded and sticking up out of the bath.

She rested her back against the smooth porcelain, taking a minute to pull out her hairpins, which she handed to him. Bryan didn't say anything, just watched her slide down until only her face and the points of her breasts were above the water.

Her hair slowly unfurled into mermaid locks that waved softly. She stared straight up at the ceiling and he looked down at her. He used a hand to adjust his cock, which was responding in a big, big way to the beautiful sight of Odette in her bath.

Eventually she rose, sleeking her hair back over her head and shivering a little.

"Please close the door," she asked him. "There is a draft."

"What? Oh, sure," he said.

"You can sit down."

He found a stool and sat, then just looked at her with awe. Just like this, with no makeup and dripping wet, she looked more beautiful than ever.

Bryan was hot and beginning to sweat. "Mind if I strip down some?" he asked.

"No."

He pulled off his top, then resumed his position on the stool. "This is great. I like my new job as goddess washer. What do you want done first?"

That got a teeny smile from her. It was a start.

"My back."

She sat up and turned around, presenting her glistening back to him. Bryan sighed and got his hands wet, then reached for the soap, lathering it up in his hands.

Odette took her hair and twisted the water out of it, then let the long twist drip over her breasts, sighing when his soaped-up hands stroked her back.

Down and down, then around in sensual circles. The soap foam dissolved in the water that lapped at her waist. Too bad he couldn't see her ass as well as before.

She enjoyed what he was doing and murmured appreciatively under her breath.

Bryan found a washcloth, soaked it, and scrubbed every sweet inch of her that he could reach. His cloth-covered hand moved under her arms and gave each breast a stimulating, sloppy rubdown.

He gritted his teeth when he saw the foam he'd created drip from one erect nipple as she leaned forward. Then her own hand came up out of the water and she twirled the soapy nipple in her fingertips. Then the other.

She closed her eyes. "It feel so good," she said softly. "It is all right to forget for a while, *n'est-ce pas?*"

"Hell fucking yes," he muttered. "Best thing you could do."

Self-serving advice, but it happened to be right. He shifted position on the stool so his straining cock wouldn't die trapped.

Odette turned toward him, raising her arms. "Do both at once," she said.

He soaped up his hands and the dripping cloth, and washed

both her breasts in slow circles, mesmerized by the foam moving over them and dissolving in the bathwater.

Then she rose to her knees and slid her fingers into her pussy, masturbating for him while he attended to her breasts. She used both hands after a little while, and the pressure of her arms made her breasts squeeze together and stick out.

If her nipples hadn't been covered in soap, he would have fastened his mouth on them and sucked her hard. He just kept rubbing. After a minute, he dropped the washcloth in the bath and sluiced her down with it when he found it again.

The fragrance of lavender and aroused woman mingled with the steam, making him giddy with desire.

He wondered if she was going to come. He wanted to watch every second of it. He'd get his chance sooner or later.

Bryan loved her like this. Purely emotional, totally sensual. Her eyes closed, the last trace of the tears she'd shed washed away, her lips parted, her face a little flushed.

The thick twist of hair over her shoulder still trickled clear water and it ran down right between her breasts and into her bellybutton.

Impulsively, Bryan bent forward and licked it up, rimming the pretty hole to nowhere with the tip of his tongue.

Odette trembled and stopped what she was doing, running her fingers into his hair instead.

"Keep masturbating," he said, rising up to catch a half kiss. "I like watching you."

"Mmm," she protested. "I will, in a moment."

She bent to pull the plug and the soapy water quickly drained. On all fours, she fiddled with the taps until she got the water going again, hotter this time, and she jammed the plug back in.

"Now that I am clean, I want to soak for a little longer."

"Whatever." He wasn't going to argue.

She rolled around like a seal, then got comfortable with a folded towel behind her neck. And spread her legs.

Under the shimmering surface of the water, Bryan watched her fingers slide into her pussy, then pull out to pinch her clit.

Odette sighed with satisfaction. "I like to know you're watching."

Watching wasn't a strong enough word. His eyes were riveted to her semi-private pleasure. He'd picked the right time to come over, that was for sure.

"But I don't want to come just yet," she was saying.

"Whatever you want, however you want it, is fine with me."

"*Bien,*" she whispered. "Now that I am very clean, I want your finger in my anus. A bit of submissiveness is good for a woman."

"If you say so."

The provocative look in her dark eyes was anything but submissive. Odette turned and got on all fours, showing him her wet behind. There were two red spots where she'd been sitting on it, and between, nestled snugly and swollen, were her labia.

Yes, he'd seen all that before, but not quite like this.

She rested her face on the folded towel and closed her eyes. He looked around for lube and found some in a basket by the bath. "Got it," he said. "You like to play like this in the bath, I take it."

"Mm-hm," she murmured, still not opening her eyes. "Sometimes I put a small toy in my behind. If I must make myself come, I want to come hard."

"How do you hold it in?" he asked, breathing hard.

"I have one that straps around my waist and up through my thighs.

"I want to see that. But first—" He put a dab of lube on her

136

squeaky-clean hole, not waiting for permission. Odette gave a little, ladylike groan as he thrust his finger in.

"There you go. Your asshole is hot, honey. Just like the rest of you."

She drew in a breath and moved to let him penetrate her a little more deeply. Her arms were folded now, pressing down on the towel as she turned her head from side to side.

"Do you have a fantasy that goes along with this?" he asked, about ready to explode in his jeans.

"Yes," she murmured. "Of a man I do not know watching me in the bath . . . then entering . . . and taking his pleasure. He uses his finger and then a dildo. Then he makes me keep it in my ass as he fucks me."

"Who's on top?"

"I am," Odette whispered. "Experiencing double penetration."

"Got it. And you're going to get it." He gave her several more skillful thrusts, enjoying her squirming.

He pulled out his finger and rinsed it, then her, rising as he gave her happy ass several stinging slaps with the wet washcloth. Odette reached down and pulled the plug, breathing fast with anticipation, not thinking of anything but sex.

Fantastic. He couldn't fix everything that had just gone wrong, but he sure as hell could take care of her physical needs. Bryan grinned and gave his hot cock a squeeze inside his jeans, leaving a wet mark on the fly.

He helped her up and gave her a raw kiss, plunging his tongue into her mouth and pressing up against her.

Odette reached down and frantically fondled his cock, moaning into the kiss.

"So where's the toy?" he asked.

She pushed him away and reached up to a cabinet, taking out a slender dildo attached to thin straps from a box.

"Put it on."

She stepped into as if she were putting on a dainty pair of panties. The dildo bobbed at the back and the head of it bumped her ass cheeks as she pulled the straps up over her hips.

"How do you—"

She took the tube of lube, twisting her body at the waist to smear some on the head.

Then she turned all the way around and bent all the way down, her behind at the level of his waist. "Spread me. Guide it in."

Her wanton pose made his breath catch but he did what she said, first finding the tiny clasp that released all the straps at once. Odette sighed as the head of the toy stretched open her anus and she groaned with deep pleasure when Bryan pushed it in.

Then she stood up again, snapping the straps that held it inside her bottom.

"Do you want to be on top?" he asked.

"Yes," she breathed, "but not here. In the bedroom."

Walking sensually—he guessed it added to her pleasure—she led the way, and he shucked the rest of his clothes in about three seconds when they got there.

Bryan stretched out on the bed. He spread his legs to ease his aching balls, then pulled on his taut scrotum as he closed them again. He rolled on the condom she handed him without taking a beat. "C'mon and ride me," he said.

His cock was so erect he had to force it to bend as she straddled him.

For the second time in five minutes he guided something into her. Only this time the head was his. Even sheathed in a tight condom, it was ultra-sensitive, wanting to get between her legs and pump, be milked by her clenching pussy . . . and rubbed through her pussy walls by the dildo in her other hole.

She pushed down on his rod and moved his hand around to

between her ass cheeks. "Fuck me in both," she moaned. "I want it double."

Beyond thinking, he just did it. His arms were long enough to reach around her easily.

Stroke for stroke, he matched her rhythm as she clutched his chest, digging her nails in, taking a hard ride on his unbelievably stiff cock and taking it in the ass from him simultaneously.

Odette began to scream under her breath with the sheer pleasure of it.

Her soft bottom tensed with each of her downward thrusts, touching and bouncing on his balls.

Bryan groaned, not able to keep from . . . ohhh . . . yes. Here it came. In thick spurts, he shot his load as she pounded even faster, rubbing the clit that the on-top position kept exposed inside her spread labia.

One of his hands stretched open to its utmost to keep the dildo rammed up inside her as she came too, bucking wildly, frantic for release.

He eased it out, fumbling for the tiny clasp that released the straps and removing the dildo as she collapsed over him. "Shhh . . . there you go," he whispered into her hair. The still-wet locks cooled his hot face. "You okay, baby?"

She nodded without speaking, burying her face against his neck as she came back to reality.

Slowly.

He had a feeling she didn't want to be back.

Bryan let her stay where she was, feeling her hot tears trickle through her wet hair onto his skin. Her body shook with sobs.

"It's okay," he said softly, stroking her back. There, she was wet with the sweat of her intense orgasm. "I'm here. It's okay." Escaping into sex was more than okay—when life really sucked, you had to go non-verbal.

The slow pulsing of his ebbing erection reminded him to get the condom safely off before he went soft and spilled his juice.

He lifted her up and kissed her nose. "Gotta deal with that," he said. Odette understood and scrambled a little awkwardly to one side.

Bryan pulled off the condom, then looked at the bedraggled, not very happy woman on the bed. "C'mon," he said. "Back to the bath. Let's wash off the sweat and then we can just cuddle."

She nodded, getting up and padding after him without saying a word.

Bryan figured a shower would be the fastest way to the cuddling she so obviously needed, so they shared a splashy one and he got her bundled up in a huge towel, drying himself vigorously before they went back to the bedroom and got under the covers.

She burrowed under his arm and he could tell she was crying again. Then she stopped and lifted her head, resting it on his chest while she brushed her fingertips lightly over the fine hair there.

"What am I going to do?" she murmured.

"We can think about that later. For now, let's get some sleep."

Next to sex, it was the best non-verbal cure for everything that he could think of.

"Put on your comfy clothes," he said when they crawled out of bed somewhere around eleven p.m. "Let's fix something we can eat on the sofa, I'll rub your feet for dessert, and then we can talk."

"What about you? I have no comfy man clothes."

"Odette, in case you haven't noticed, I'm an all-American slob. All my clothes are comfortable."

She made a funny little face. "But sexy, though."

"Thanks."

"I did notice you had no interest in fashion," she said with a sigh. "It is one reason I have to trust you."

Bryan stiffened and looked at her warily. "Only one? You didn't think that I had anything to do with stealing your designs, did you?"

"No. But the investigator did ask."

He scowled. "Has someone been following me around? I assume for a case this size he doesn't work alone."

"Not as far as I know. But yes, he does have a team."

Bryan imagined them in wraparound sunglasses and well-cut suits, looking cynical and dashing around Paris, screaming at all the people they ran over to get out of the way.

"Anyway, he wanted to know if I'd met someone new, and he asked about, as he put it, other changes in my life."

"I hope you didn't give him the play-by-play and post-game analysis."

"What is that?" Odette asked.

"Sports talk. I meant what we do in bed."

"Ah, no. Certainly not. I only told him that you were the raffle ticket winner and I suppose he took it from there. There was an article on line right away and everything you told me about yourself checked out, as far as he could tell."

"That really doesn't give me the warm fuzzies."

"And what are those?" Odette wanted to know.

"Good feelings. Like when you're safe and all is right with the world. The way I'm trying to make you feel right now."

She looked at him worriedly. "Forgive me. I am trying to be honest about the investigator and since you were right there when I was fitting Grischenka—"

"I wasn't exactly thinking straight, believe me."

"Why not?"

"Uh, there was a lot going on? Such as you kneeling in front of her shaved pussy and Lucie joining you on the floor? Then the petals getting plucked off Grischenka's bare skin? The three of you made my balls turn bright blue."

Odette seemed piqued. "Did you find her attractive?"

"Yes and no."

"Explain, *s'il vous plait.*"

Bryan hesitated. It didn't seem possible that a CEO of an international unmentionables business could get her own undies in a twist over something like that, but by the expression on her face, he guessed that she was.

"Um, you invited me to look on, Odette. Let's keep that in mind."

"Are you saying that I am responsible for you being attracted to Grischenka?"

"I didn't say I was attracted to her, did I?"

"No, but—"

Bryan blew out an exasperated breath. This discussion was likely to turn into a pointless fight and he was hungry. "Grischenka is nine feet tall, spooky-looking, probably not very bright, and she has no ass."

"You must have liked something about her."

"That is a trick question."

Odette sniffed. "You can answer it all the same."

"She had perfect tits. Maybe too perfect, but—"

"I knew it!" Odette crowed. "So you think they were nicer than mine? You are a pig!" She made a Gallic gesture that he had to assume meant something like go *fuck yourself* or *jump in the Seine* or both.

"Once again, I didn't say that. And I plead not guilty to the pig part of the accusation. I answered your question honestly and like a man."

"Hmf." She sulked but Bryan did detect a slight softening in her tone. "Very well, man," she said at last. "Perhaps we should not quarrel, eh?"

He relaxed. Just a little.

"It isn't going to get us anywhere, Odette."

She screwed up her mouth as she deliberated that reasonable question. "I suppose not."

"Then can we eat?"

"*Bien sûr.*" She headed into the kitchen, and clattered around. Wonderful smells soon emanated from the region as Bryan headed for the relative safety of the sofa.

She probably needed to eat too. With a good dinner rounding her flat belly a little and a glass of wine, he would rub her feet and get the rest of the story out of her.

Eventually she came back out with steaming bowls of chicken. New potatoes and other small vegetables kept it company.

Bryan sniffed appreciatively. "Smells great."

"It is nothing special," she said. "*Coq au vin.* And speaking of *vin*, you may uncork the bottle on the table."

He jumped up with alacrity and did the honors. "Are you sure we can manage eating that on the sofa? We could light some candles and eat here." He found two wineglasses and filled them, setting them on the table.

"How romantic," she said flatly.

"Yeah. It is romantic. Are you crabby because you had to cook?"

Odette tried to hide a guilty smile. "I wish I could make that excuse. But this is from Bonne Femme. Peasant cooking without the peasant."

"Is that their slogan?"

"Yes." Odette brought the two bowls over to the table. "All right. We can eat here."

"You still get a foot rub."

She nodded, looking pleased as she slid into her seat.

"Got any bread?" he asked.

"You are turning into a Frenchman," she remarked. "In the kitchen. There is a half a baguette. It is a little stale but will be good in the broth."

He found it and tore off chunks for both of them on his way back. She tore hers into smaller pieces and floated them in her soup, and he did the same.

"Okay, no more talking. Bad for the digestion."

She sipped at a spoonful of broth. Just that little taste seemed to do her good. He dug in and they ate heartily. Bryan took care of the dishes, since the takeout place didn't provide a peasant to wash them, and then joined her on the sofa.

She was covered up in a blanket by the time he got there. But her toes were sticking out.

"Ready for me, Madame Gaillard?" he asked.

Odette gave him a morose look. "Must you call me Madame? It sounds old."

"Sorry. I won't. We never did swap life stories," he said, getting settled and lifting one of her bare feet into his lap. "But I guess you got most of mine from the article. I don't even know how old you are. And I don't care."

"Twenty-nine," she said gloomily.

"I'm twenty-five."

"Marc thought at first that you were too young for me."

Bryan began to make slow circles into her arch with the pad of his thumb. "He's protective of you, Odette."

She raised an eyebrow. "Have you two been talking about me?"

"Uh, we ran into each other. Yeah, your name came up."

"Hmm. I'm not sure I like that."

Bryan went a little deeper, intensifying the sensation. He

gave killer foot rubs. She might as well get used to them for the time they had together.

"But I do like that—I mean what you are doing," she was saying. "Ahhmmm—ohh. There. Very good. Anyway, what did he say and what did you say?"

"That's between us guys. Is talking about Your You-ness not allowed, oh queen?"

Odette raised her foot to give him a little kick but he got a grip on her ankle.

"Let's change the subject. What does the investigator think happened? And what is the guy's name, anyway?"

"Herman Goffre. He believes that it was an inside job."

"Why?" He moved his caressing thumb to the ball of her foot and stayed there for a while.

"Because corporate espionage usually is. Someone is paid to provide secrets, often someone who holds a grudge against the company for some reason, or thinks they are underpaid and that they deserve the extra money. Or that's how Goffre explained it."

"Which is another reason he decided not to suspect me, I guess. I'm just your boy toy."

Odette shook her head. "He did want to know how long you were staying in Paris."

"Oh yeah. I was wondering when we would get around to that."

"And what is the answer?" She sighed while she was waiting to hear it. "I wish I had four feet. Or six. Or eight. You could massage them all and I could die of pleasure."

"Isn't that what the French call an orgasm? The little death?"

"Yes, that is the expression." She gave him a slightly embarrassed grin. "I experienced one this afternoon. You seem to know exactly what I want."

"You give very clear instructions, Odette."

She sighed and arched her foot as he moved to her heel, rubbing a little harder there. Then she jerked and giggled. "A reflex. Continue."

"Like I said. You know what you want."

"Perhaps, Bryan. But you do seem to have an instinctive understanding of women."

He gave an unconcerned shrug. "I have a degree in biology. Sex is next to breathing for most species."

"But you are a marine biologist."

"Yeah, so?"

"Fish—cannot be passionate."

"You'd be surprised. Even the invertebrates get crazy." He moved his thumb in swooping motions from her heel to just under her toes, gathering up the tension and pressing it out. "There are sea slugs who can switch genders."

"How ingenious of them."

"They have to be ingenious. Have you ever seen one?"

"Only once," she murmured. "In the Chinese market. Dead. Dried. It was revolting."

"Well, if it was living and rolling around seductively on the ocean floor, another sea slug would think it was hot. Anyway, they double their chances by being hermaphroditic."

"Oh, of course," she said, laughing. "Do you know, Marc once took me to a club where—" She obeyed her own command and pressed her lips together like she knew a secret she wasn't going to tell. "Never mind."

Bryan put down the foot he'd been working on and picked up the other. "I take it you didn't go to see naked slugs."

Her eyes danced. "Ask him to bring you there."

He nodded. "Okay, I will. While we're on the subject, I guess I should tell you I checked out of the hotel. I happened to meet Marc when I left the atelier—" He caught her dubious look and added, "True story. He's really concerned about you, thought it would be a good idea if I stuck around, since I don't have to return to the U.S., and he invited me to stay at his place."

"I see."

"It'll save a little money." He still didn't feel like explaining his finances to her. "I can change the date on my ticket."

"I will cover that," Odette said.

"No. But thanks. Anyway, they live in the Marais—I guess you know that. And I met Achille and Jimmy."

"*Zut.* Who is Jimmy? Marc believes in fidelity and romance. I cannot imagine him in a *ménage a trois.*"

"Jimmy is a Chihuahua. The smallest one I've ever seen but he knows how to throw his weight around. He fits in the pocket of Achille's coat."

"Ah, he must be a new acquisition." Her face lit up with a fond smile. "Marc and Achille are like a married couple."

"I got that impression."

She surrendered to his stroking for a little while. "Well, so you have a temporary home. You could have stayed with me."

"Best to give each other room to breathe, don't you think? Especially when we get each other as hot as we do."

"You are probably right. But I would have invited you had I known—"

"It worked out fine. Let's leave things as they are."

Odette gave him a mischievous look. "Marc will keep an eye on you for more reasons than one."

"I don't even want to know."

"First, because you and I are lovers," Odette went on, disregarding his protest, "and second, because you are handsome."

"Aw, shucks."

He stopped for a moment and she took the opportunity to

pull her feet back under the blanket. "It feels wonderful but I cannot think when you do that. And I have to think."

"Right. Let's get back to that."

"But first tell me where you learned to give such sexy massages."

"Foot rubs are more therapeutic than sexy."

She studied him for a long moment. "You are dodging my question."

"Okay, okay." He threw up his hands, now that he had nothing to do with them. "An ex-girlfriend taught me. She was a masseuse. Ayurvedic oils, hot stones, shiatsu—she did it all. She was an expert."

"A loving one?"

"She practiced on me." He gave her the short version of the rest of it. "Nice girl. She fell in love with her guru, an old guy—talk about sea slugs." He grinned when Odette laughed. "Anyway, he told me that she needed to move on. You learn."

Odette shook her head. "I wonder who taught whom. Your touch has a special quality. Perhaps the secret is emotional rapport—" She stopped and giggled when he picked up her foot and pretended to snack on her toes.

"The secret is not stopping. I like having you literally in the palm of my hand, Odette."

"Do you?"

Her voice was so wistful that he turned to her in surprise. "It's just an expression. But yeah—I do."

She moved the blanket and crawled over to get next to him, pulling it over both of them. "I feel so peaceful with you. Like we could just shut out the world and be together."

"Yeah?" He stroked her hair, looking around her apartment. "We're from really different worlds, though."

"But—"

148

"Let's not talk about it."

"Sorry." She gave him a playful bite. "I am in a sentimental mood and I let my guard down. I am never going to let you touch my feet again."

"So long as I can get my hands on the rest of you—" he broke off to slide his hands around whatever curve was nearest and gave her a long, deep kiss. Even in the middle of it, he told himself not to get used to this.

He was kissing a beautiful Frenchwoman who made the best takeout food in the world. He was caught up in a mystery he might be able to help solve that involved naked models and no dead bodies. Given a chance to be a hero for Odette, he'd take it. By sheer chance, he was staying in Paris longer than he'd expected and not as a tourist, but with interesting, sophisticated people who weren't snooty to him, even though he dressed like a hang-ten jock and ate BLTs. The sunny state of California seemed hella far away.

This won't last, he told himself. He stopped the endless smooch by mixing in a bunch of little ones, kissing her ear, her cheek, her hair, her neck, until she begged happily for mercy.

"Okay, Mademoiselle Velcro," he said with mock sternness. "We do have to finish talking about the design theft. When we walk out of here tomorrow, you'll still have to deal with it. And I don't want to be accused of distracting you."

She sat up. "All right then. I am meeting again with the investigator tomorrow, so you are right. You are a distraction. Never in my life have I been so distracted."

Bryan waved that away. "Not your fault. Women all over the globe beg for my company."

"Pah."

"Getting back to the investigator, does he have a plan or anything?"

Odette nodded. "He intends to check out everyone who works for me, within the limits of the law. I told him to start with the people who were there that day."

"Me, for one. I was taking pictures."

"Yes, I remember. I borrowed your camera and took some myself. Of Grischenka."

He hadn't thought of it since. "Is Goffre going to think that I stole your designs?"

"Of course not. I will explain. I know it stayed in your possession until Lucie told me to come look at what she found."

He thought it over. "Hey, I could do a download and you could forward them to the guy from here."

"Really?"

Bryan shook his head. "Wait a minute. I forgot I left the camera at Marc's apartment and it's miles away. Besides, it's late."

"I will text him tomorrow morning and tell him to bring it with him."

"Sounds like a plan. Or I can call him, if you have to leave early. You don't want to show up at work with me, do you?"

She shrugged. "Why not? It is not a big secret that we met at the show and people can think whatever they want."

"Yeah, but under the circumstances, your staff is going to wonder why I'm not being investigated."

"They won't hear it from me."

"Even so," he said firmly. "I don't really want to walk in like I own the place all of a sudden."

Bryan tried to remember where he'd left the camera—it was small and a little too easy to lose. "My stuff's in the Moroccan chest. If you reach Marc before I do, you can tell him it's okay to look through it."

"Okay. I took notes while Goffre was talking. Do you want to see them?"

"Sure."

She got up and went to fetch her purse, pulling out a notebook bound in vinyl, which she opened as she settled back down, reading through them. "Blah blah . . . and blah blah blah. I think I have told you all this already."

Bryan nodded and came to sit by her. "I remember who I saw there, but if you want to know their names, it's going to be a short list: Lucie, Delphine, and Marc. All the people in the cubicles smiled and waved—I took a few shots of some of them."

"Not of the designs, of course."

"No. You told me not to. I even asked a couple of people to move things like sketches so I wouldn't snap 'em by accident."

"It will be interesting to see those photos."

Bryan hemmed and hawed a little. "I guess. But it's not like anyone's going to have a little sign over their head that says GUILTY."

"No, I suppose not."

"How much is this investigator guy charging you?"

She told him and he whistled. "No kidding. He'd better come up with something."

"Yes. Before I lose my Japanese client. That account alone is worth millions."

"So you said." He drew in his breath, then let it out again. "Maybe talking about it isn't such a great idea. You won't be able to fall asleep."

"Ah, Bryan. You can help me with that."

He pulled her close. "Ready for seconds?"

"Yes. You are a magic man."

8

_____

The next morning he was back at Marc's apartment, playing with Jimmy while Marc made coffee.

"Achille is at the markets still," he called from the kitchen. "He prowls through before dawn to get the best vegetables and meat and fish. Then he comes home to sleep."

"Not a problem. I'll be gone by then." Bryan found a ping-pong ball with tiny toothmarks in it wedged under the sofa. "Is this yours?" he asked Jimmy. He threw it, and it bounced once and stopped rolling. The little dog could barely get his jaws around the smooth white sphere but he managed. He sat down with it in his mouth, looking triumphant.

For a full minute.

"Is this what Mexican stand-off means?" Bryan finally asked the dog.

"What?" Marc called.

"I was talking to Jimmy. Does he understand the other half of the fetch equation?"

"No," Marc said, coming into the room and sipping coffee from a mug. "Jimmy, smile for papa."

The Chihuahua curled up his lips but didn't release the ball.

"Not like that," Marc reproved him. "You look evil, to say nothing of disgusting. You look like an egg-sucking, four-legged snake and not a dog."

The insults had no effect.

"Papa is not proud of you," Marc added.

Giving both men a look of chagrin, Jimmy finally dropped the ball and Bryan threw it again. The ball went into a corner, where the dog ran and snuffled around for it.

"All right," Marc sighed. "Enough of this. I have to get to work."

Bryan nodded.

"Are you going to the atelier?"

"Not just yet. Making an, uh, separate entrance."

Marc shrugged. "We assumed you spent the night with Odette. That is probably a wise thing to do—arrive at different times, I mean."

"We thought so."

Marc seemed to approve of that. "Well, she ought to be calmer today, lover boy. Am I right?"

Bryan felt his face turn red. "I can't speak for her."

The other man laughed in a friendly way. "Still, I am sure you did her good. And I am grateful. Goffre is coming in to interview us, one by one."

"Odette mentioned it."

"Am I a suspect?" Marc asked calmly.

"She told me right from the start that you were the only person on her staff that she totally trusted."

The other man gave a shrug. "Goffre might not agree."

"I don't think you're on the list," Bryan said.

"So there is a list. Are you on it, Bryan?"

He shook his head. "She seems to trust me too."

"Then Goffre will gnash his teeth in frustration." Marc

drank down his coffee. "What can he do, eh? The designs are worthless. Snatched from under Odette's nose. She will never profit from them."

"That sucks."

"Yes. But it happens." Marc rummaged in the closet for his jacket, pulling out several before he found the one he wanted. "Fashion changes so quickly it almost does not matter. We have to present six or seven collections a year now. Five was hard enough—"

"That many?"

"Used to be only four." Marc shrugged into his jacket. "Craziness. Where is my cell phone?" He looked around and saw it on the mantel because it was blinking. "Aha. A message. Somebody loves me. Who can it be?" He looked at the screen. "Odette."

Bryan watched as he read the text message she'd left, just then remembering about the camera.

"She says you took pictures?" Marc asked.

"Yeah. I have to get them on a disk. Is there a drugstore around here?"

"There is a photo store two blocks away. May I look at them first?" Marc asked.

"Sure. I think they're in the chest." Jimmy was right in front of it. "Excuse me, pup." He squatted down and moved the little dog to one side.

He found the camera and handed it over. "Press the button, hit the arrow. The usual."

Marc had it figured out already. "Okay. I understand." He scrolled through the pictures. "There are our worker bees, busy as usual in their cells. Nothing out of the ordinary."

"I just wanted to snap a few for my mom. Odette told me not to take pictures of any sketches or projects, so I concentrated on the people."

"Nice one of Delphine," Marc commented.

"We chatted when I went to get coffee."

"And here is Lucie. So efficient. And so dedicated," the other man murmured. "She knows how to do nearly everything."

"She was helping Odette with the model fitting for the flower-petal underwear."

"Yes, she is clever at such things. I don't know what Odette would do without her."

"And here is Grischenka. Did you take those?"

"No. Odette did. I was too weak."

Marc laughed loudly. "Grischenka is a bit of a freak, but men notice her."

"She's hard to miss."

Marc hummed as he scrolled back, looking at all the photos again. Bryan heard a faint whirring noise as the other man pressed the zoom button on the viewfinder.

"That is interesting," he said softly.

"What?" Bryan said, standing as he came over to look.

"The papers in her purse. I can't quite see it, even with the zoom."

Bryan looked. Pieces of paper were sticking out of the capacious purse just in back of Lucie. He couldn't make out anything.

"Hmm," Marc said at last. "Odette wanted me to bring this to the investigator, but I think I would like a friend of mine to look at it first. With your permission," he added, handing the camera back to Bryan.

"Okay," Bryan said. "I wasn't going to be interviewed by the guy."

"I will tell Odette that you couldn't find it," Marc said. "But on second thought, do not take it to the photo store. I would rather my friend downloads that picture directly."

"Uh—okay. What's going on?"

156

Marc shrugged. "Until we get a better look at what is in Lucie's purse, that is hard to say."

"Oh. Should I tell Odette?"

"Not yet. She relies on Lucie nearly as much as she relies on me. I don't want to make her nervous."

"So long as she gets a full report if there is anything." Bryan was relieved that he had the camera in hand.

"Of course. *Au revoir,* Jimmy." Marc bent down to pat the little dog. "Bryan will walk you later. His leash is hanging by the back door," he said to Bryan.

"Okay. Sure thing."

He let Jimmy curl up next to his ankle as he looked through the photos he'd taken on the viewfinder again, studying the one of Lucie that had caught Marc's eye.

No matter how close he got in, the paper in her purse looked blank to him.

The hell with it, he decided.

"Do you want to go out tonight?" Marc had come home and was preparing supper.

Bryan thought of Odette's laughing over the club her assistant had taken her to, and her refusal to say anything much about it.

"Where to?" he said cautiously.

"A club called Vendredi. It is open every night of the week, but on Thursdays it gets really interesting."

"In what way? If you don't mind my asking." Bryan reminded himself that he was a guest.

"Everyone comes."

That answer was not informative. He couldn't remember if Odette had told him the name of the place. Vendredi wasn't ringing a bell.

Even so.

How bad could it be? Since he wasn't paying for a hotel, he had a few bucks left for an evening out with the, uh, guys.

"Achille goes to bed early so it will be just you and me."

That seemed more doable, somehow, especially since he knew Marc a little.

"Sure," he said at last. "I'd love to go."

Marc hummed as he chopped vegetables. "It is inexpensive."

Nice of Marc to assume that was what had been on his mind, Bryan thought. He felt a little ashamed of himself for being nervous.

Still, being laid back had its drawbacks, such as saying yes to things he didn't really want to do. He hoped Vendredi wasn't going to be too weird.

Achille came home and banged the door open. "Where's my supper?" he howled.

"Oh, shut up," Marc said pleasantly. "You can see that I'm making it."

Odette was right. Marc and his boyfriend really were married. Achille showered as Marc set the table for three, still humming. The food was delicious, beef in sauce enriched with red wine. And there was more red wine to drink.

"Oh," Marc said causally, "we will be meeting a friend of mine tonight who can help us get a better look at that picture. She is the only person I know who has the right software, and I don't want to—" He broke off, then went on. "If you bring the camera and the connector, she will bring her laptop."

"Should we be doing this in public?"

"She works two jobs and sleeps during the day. She is a computer programmer and an entertainer."

"Oh, you mean like a comedian? I know a couple of geek stand-up comics. They do *Dilbert*-type stuff."

"She is not a comedian. But she is a wizard with software."

"Couldn't you have Odette's computer guys handle this?"

"I don't want to seem as if—as if I am making an accusation against a person on Odette's staff. Jeanne can be trusted—I have known her ever since—" He stopped. "I have known her for a long time. So she is doing me a favor."

"All right. I see." He kind of didn't.

Marc shrugged. "It is just a preliminary look to see if there is a clue worth pursuing. We will have a private booth at the club."

Bryan wasn't sure if the private booth or the photo thing made him more nervous.

"Uh, okay."

He poured himself another glass and so did Marc, then helped him clear the table and do the dishes.

Achille went out to walk the dog and came back with it in his pocket, yapping at them.

Bryan patted the Chihuahua and its skinny little tail thumped inside the canvas pocket. "Have a nice ride?"

"He walked almost a block," Achille said, lifting his pet out and putting him on the floor.

"A record for that dog," Marc sniffed. He opened up another bottle of wine, and set out cheese and fruit.

Nice place. Nice guys. Nice Chihuahua. Bryan was feeling no pain by the time they finished the second bottle, said goodnight to Achille and went outside to walk to the club.

The night air was cold and Bryan didn't mind having a buzz on. He nodded to the old lady at the door, and walked inside with Marc.

They slid into a booth and ordered drinks, then Marc leaned across the booth's table. "My friend will be here in a little while. The show is about to begin."

Bryan leaned back and looked at the small stage. A gorgeous, heavily made-up girl came on, not wearing a whole hell of a lot otherwise. He smiled lazily. All right. So far it reminded him of Odette's show, except this girl was voluptuous up top.

She bounced and preened and flirted with the guys in the front row. Bryan couldn't quite suss out the vibe of the place.

Why Marc, who was gay, would go to a club with female entertainers wasn't clear to him.

Because she was female. He wasn't so smashed he couldn't tell the difference. He squinted at the stage and hoped he was right.

Whatever. Marc, the true believer in true love, wasn't going to buy him a lap dance if he thought Odette needed Bryan and vice versa.

Bryan closed his eyes, feeling the stronger drink on top of the red wine, as well as the effects of not sleeping all that much.

The eagerness of the men down front and the growing hubbub as the place filled up drifted over him. He opened his eyes when Marc touched his arm.

There was a woman at the table with him. Someone in serious horn rims with her hair cut just above her shoulders. Not young, not old. She reminded him of his high school guidance counselor. He half expected her to wave college brochures under his nose and talk about what he wanted to do with his life.

Instead she took a laptop out of a padded bag, and opened the lid.

"Bryan, this is my friend Jeanne," Marc said. "Jeanne, this is Bryan."

No last names. Fine with Bryan, who struggled to sit upright. He wasn't quite sure he should be doing this anyway.

"You did bring the camera?"

"Yes," he said, smiling at Jeanne. "I guess Marc explained this to you. We're trying to get a better look at a photo I took."

She nodded seriously. "He did explain. I have pixel-enhancing software." She patted her laptop.

"All right. Marc, do you think I could get some coffee?"

Marc nodded and signaled the waiter over, giving him the order.

The girl on stage was introducing performers one by one for what looked like it was going to be a burlesque-style revue. Heat level: Rotary Club. Bryan stifled a yawn. This wasn't going to be a night to remember. Good. He would rather make memories with Odette.

He took the camera and its connector out of his pocket and handed it to Jeanne, who hooked it up and downloaded the images.

She scrolled through them. "As you said, Marc. They seem quite ordinary."

"One is different."

"Stop me when I get to it," Jeanne said. "Wait. Is that Grischenka?"

"Yes. Odette was doing a fitting on her. For the flower panties." He deflected her inquiring look with a wave of his hand. "The design is all over the internet. We have kissed it good-bye forever."

"Hmm," Jeanne said. "I suppose that did seem too obvious to have photos of it and the owner of the camera sitting right here." She smiled at Bryan. "It is not as if I am a detective and can arrest you."

"Nope." He smiled back. Okay, she wasn't a detective, but who was she? And why did Marc want her to digitally enhance the photos without telling Odette? Something wasn't adding up.

The raucous show on stage got louder. Bryan drank the coffee the waiter brought for him but it didn't do much to clear his mind.

"That one," Marc said, putting his hand on Jeanne's arm.

"Ah. I see a woman's shoulder and a purse behind her."

"Zoom in on the purse. And then enhance the pixels."

She sighed and muttered something about visual noise, then got to work.

"I see what you mean," she said to Marc. "There is an address on it."

"Can it be read?"

She clicked on more keys. "I will try a different function of the software. The problem is that the piece of paper is not straight up and down. The image is tilted. I have to correct for anamorphic distortion."

Her plain face looked a little ghostly in the blue light of the monitor. Bryan could see the purse part of the photo reflected in her glasses, could even watch her zoom in on the piece of paper, making it move around in various ways.

Marc leaned closer, looking over her shoulder.

"I have it," she said suddenly. "There is an address on it. Look."

"Yes," Marc said slowly, reading it. "I thought there might be."

"Why?" Bryan waited for him to explain.

"I noticed the piece of paper that day when I walked by Lucie's cubicle, but not what was on it," Marc replied. "She knows I can be fussy about hers being in a mess. She saw me coming, crammed the paper into her purse, and put the purse under her desk. I didn't really think about it," he said to Jeanne. "Then, after everything happened, Bryan showed me the photos he'd taken and I realized he'd taken them while the paper was still sticking out. There was just something odd about the way she was acting. I think now she was making sure I couldn't read it."

"Then why did she have it out where anyone could see it in the first place?" Bryan asked.

"She was distracted. Or busy." He glanced up and caught Bryan's mystified look. "As I told you, Odette thinks that Lucie can do no wrong, but I am not so sure."

"Don't you sell to New York?" He tried to remember the names of the stores. One, from his mother's fashion magazines, came to mind. "Like Saks Fifth Avenue or something?"

"No. We sell all over the world but we are not yet in New York stores. So why would Lucie have this address?"

"Could be a friend of hers," Bryan said. Marc's reasoning seemed far-fetched.

"Not on the corner of 39th and Seventh Avenue."

"I'm not following you."

"That is the heart of the garment district. There may be a few lofts but not many. No, it is mostly manufacturers of cheaper goods. Fabric stores. Button sellers. Feathers and frippery."

"Oh," Bryan said. He sort of got it.

"Anyway, Jeanne thought it might be visible if the image could be manipulated. And she was right."

"It is hard to read," Jeanne said.

Bryan scooted his chair around, suddenly intrigued and feeling a lot more awake.

Touching different keys, Jeanne made the image of the paper tilt forward so he could read it too. He could just make out the scrawled address of King Khong Fancy Goods on West 39th Street. New York, NY.

Marc gave an angry sigh as he looked at it again. "Khong. I should have known."

"It says King Khong," Bryan pointed out. "Is this a joke? Are we going to have to climb up the Empire State Building to catch him?"

Marc sat back. "I'll explain tomorrow. You and I will meet with Odette. Jeanne, please forward that to me."

"*Bien sûr.*" She clicked on a button to save the enhanced

image. "This dump has wireless, believe it or not. I could send it to you right now."

"Security is not an issue. But you can send it to me later. I won't need it until tomorrow."

"May I also save these of Grischenka?"

"If you like." Marc folded his arms across his chest. "She is going to perform here tonight." He cast a bored look toward the stage.

The voluptuous performers were grinding away, shaking their big boobs at the rowdy customers egging them on.

Bryan was baffled. "Grischenka is not in their league, man."

"No. She's had it all done."

"You lost me again, dude."

Marc didn't answer right away, waving toward someone who'd just come in. Bryan turned to look.

A extremely tall, white-blond woman in vinyl boots that came up over her knees and vinyl hot pants walked through the front part of the club.

"Here she is now," Marc said. "Grischy! Over here."

She made her way through her admirers, fending off an occasional hand on her long, long legs.

Then she sat down, expressionless somehow despite her smile. She nodded to Marc and kissed Jeanne on both cheeks.

"I have pictures of you in your pretty panties," Jeanne said to Grischenka, looking to Marc. "Still okay to show these?"

"Go ahead."

The lanky model leaned in and looked at her photos without much interest. "This is one of the stolen designs, isn't it? Too fucking bad for Odette. She wants to be a girl Gaultier and she can't."

Bryan looked at her. That was a long speech from someone who hadn't uttered any other word in his presence besides *da*. So she did talk. Too bad she didn't have anything sympathetic to say about Odette. He felt pissed at himself for ever thinking Grischenka's boobs were perfect and even worse about looking down her panties and imagining things.

"Yes. Most unfortunate," Jeanne said.

"Odette is full of stolen ideas herself," Grischenka replied in a flat voice. "She will come up with more designs and she will be more careful next time. Is the matter under investigation, Marc?"

"Of course. For what it is worth. The designs cannot be retrieved and they are not copyrighted. Nothing will come of it."

She nodded and turned away from them, draping her lanky arms over the back of her chair and watching the show as if she'd seen it a thousand times before.

"Why not?" Bryan asked.

"Because nothing is secret. We all live and die on the fucking internet. I need a drink." Marc signaled a passing waiter.

"Okay," Bryan interrupted, speaking a voice too low for Grischenka to hear. "Excuse me for sounding completely naïve, but why is Odette spending money on an investigation then?"

"Ah. That is actually an intelligent question. To prevent it from happening in future, if at all possible. And to satisfy her insurers."

Bryan nodded. That made a little more sense. "So now what?"

"We kiss the girls good-night and go home."

Jeanne had shut off her laptop, and stood up, along with Grischenka. They were chatting as they watched the show, out of earshot of them.

"Jeanne has to be onstage in five minutes."

"Her?" Bryan was genuinely amazed. "She does that?" He looked at the gyrating lineup of busty dancers.

Marc glanced at Jeanne. "She has the biggest of all."

"I don't mean to be rude, but I don't think she does. And Grischenka sure as hell doesn't. I've seen her with nothing on."

Marc only nodded and looked back at the stage, then his watch. "Do you want to leave before the grand finale?"

Bryan looked at the stage too, just in time to see the girls unzip their crotches and pull out what looked like real, live penises.

"Chicks with dicks." Marc yawned. "Male to female, half-way to the finish line. They do not interest me."

Bryan swallowed hard. "Me either." But he looked anyway.

The leader of the revue dangled her mighty dong and shook her boobs. Grischenka and Jeanne watched, commenting on the action.

"So she"—Bryan looked at the tall model—"used to be a he."

"As I said, she has been completely done."

"And Jeanne?"

"Has the biggest. Those girls just warm up the crowd for her."

Bryan opened his mouth and closed it again. "And you say her other job is computer programming?"

"Yes. It is amusing, no?"

"And I thought Grischenka had perfect tits. And that she was female."

Marc gave him a wink. "Boys will be girls. And girls will be boys."

"No. I mean, it's cool if you like it, but I'll take Odette."

"But of course," Marc said. "She is a true goddess. You ought to worship Odette. She deserves nothing less."

"I'm trying, man." He got to his feet, looking everywhere but at the stage. "Let's go." Jeanne and Grischenka were walking arm in arm toward the back of the club.

Bryan didn't even want to know what was going to happen next.

* * *

NIGHTS IN BLACK LACE

As it turned, not the worst.

Waking from a sleep induced by still more red wine, he felt tiny legs clasping his ankle. He shook Jimmy off.

Molested by a Chihuahua. He rubbed his aching head. It was almost funny, considering what he'd seen that night.

9

"So Khong is back in business. Are you sure?" Odette asked Marc.

"Lucie had his address in her purse. That is the only thing I know for sure. I sent you the enhanced image."

Bryan didn't know what to say or do. He was hoping for an explanation or two.

"Lucie is such a hard worker. Always putting in overtime—" She stopped herself.

Marc raised an eyebrow.

"And now we know why," Odette sighed.

"We will need more evidence before we accuse her of anything."

"The designs were reproduced somewhere in China."

Odette looked at Bryan. "Piracy is a huge problem in fashion, especially there. It happens sometimes that copies are manufactured by the same companies that make the real goods."

"Oh."

"Khong has paid millions in fines but he always pops back up. He put a friend of mine out of business with his cheap copies.

Flooded the market, then the trends changed. Poof. End of friend."

She turned back to Marc, resting her hands on the fat ring binder on her desk. "I guarded this so carefully. I thought sketches would be stolen from here." Then she tapped her temple. "It was done so quickly that it felt like they were taken from my brain."

"Lucie could have drawn your fitting session concepts from memory, scanned them, and sent them," Marc said. "And there were others that you had on paper."

"Yes." She was silent and so were the two men.

Bryan remembered Lucie's noisy indignation. "She really tried to distract you, Odette."

"I remember," she sighed crossly. "But I would rather she didn't know, Marc, that we are looking into this."

"You mean you want her to continue?" her assistant asked.

Odette nodded. "She has inadvertently provided us with Khong's address."

"Or is deliberately leading us on a wild-goose chase."

"Hmm." Odette chewed her lip, looking so sad that Bryan wanted nothing more than to take her in his arms and make this whole fucked-up situation disappear.

He couldn't. He felt worse than useless and definitely out of his element. He didn't belong here and none of this had anything to do with him.

How long would it be before she realized that herself?

He studied her unhappy, beautiful face as she chewed on her pencil. Then again, opposites attracted, at least on TV. But not even in *Le O.C.* did a poor surfer-slash-marine biologist fall in love with a French fashion designer.

It just wasn't going to happen. Or last.

She gave him a warm look from those goddamn eyes of hers, green shot with gold, and he melted inside.

It had happened. It might last.

He couldn't say the hell with it and climb on the next plane, and not only because he couldn't afford to change his ticket.

No, something like love had a hold on him and wasn't letting go. He wanted to let it happen. Just be Californian, he told himself. Go with the flow.

"Bryan, what do you think?" she asked.

"Odette, I'm really not qualified to hand out advice. I have no idea. Talk to Marc. Or the investigator guy."

She sighed. "Marc, for the moment we will keep what we know about Lucie to ourselves."

"Besides us, only Jeanne knows," he said.

"And we both know Jeanne." She and Marc shared a smile.

Bryan looked from one to the other as they did. She knew Jeanne too? Just how kinky and convoluted was this going to get?

"I met her at Vendredi last night," Marc said. "Bryan came along."

"Ah." Odette's blasé tone surprised Bryan, who told himself he shouldn't be surprised by anything people at the uppermost level of fashion did. Decadence was the new ordinary.

"Was she performing?" he heard her ask.

"No, I missed that part."

Marc smirked and Bryan turned red at his unintentional double entendre.

"It is not the sort of part one can miss," Marc pointed out.

"Give it a rest, pal," Bryan said, annoyed with him. He was going to have to ask Odette a few questions when her assistant was elsewhere. But in the meantime, he had one for both of them. "Where's Lucie, by the way?"

"Down in the stock room, comparing fabric samples to the Pantone colors for the season. It's donkey work," Marc said. "But she didn't complain about it."

"Do you think she knows that we know—" Bryan broke off, not certain what they *did* know for sure, besides that Lucie'd had an address tucked into her purse.

"Probably not. Lucie started out with Odette by helping to choose fabric."

Odette sighed. "I came up with a reason to have her do it now. Not a very good one, but as Marc said, she didn't complain."

"Is the plan to wait and see if she trips up?"

"I am not sure," Odette said. "For now it's best if Lucie has nothing to do with design development."

"Makes sense." The situation would need to be resolved somehow and Odette didn't waste any time. But he liked her for not getting angry and firing Lucie on the spot.

Even with a huge order on the line and millions at stake, she kept her cool.

He tapped his foot a little impatiently as Odette went over some other business quickly with Marc, who exited after that.

She stuck the spreadsheets into the binder and turned her full attention to Bryan. "Shall I have coffee sent in?"

"Fine with me. I don't have anything else to do this morning."

"How did you like the club?"

"It was . . . " He hesitated, searching his mind for the right word. "Unique."

"Some of the performers are quite entertaining. I find gender bending very amusing. And you?"

"Not so much."

She swiveled in her chair and leaned back with her hands in the armrests. She looked every inch the lady boss this morning. It was all about her attitude and not her clothes, which were interesting as usual. She wore white patent leather ankle boots, black lace stockings, a polka dot skirt, plaid blouse, and a snood. He was pretty sure that crocheted thing on her hair was called a snood.

"Why not?"

"Don't get me wrong. I have nothing against chicks with dicks. Maybe it was more the bozos down front screaming their heads off. They're pretty obnoxious."

"They are not so very different from the man we had to bounce at my show, are they?"

He wanted to roll his eyes but he didn't. He heard enough of the men-are-scum routine from Miss Peace And Love, the girl-friend who'd ditched him for another dude. A really old dude. "Whatever. It just wasn't my scene, Odette. You could have warned me."

She gave a tiny sigh of regret. "Oh well. I didn't."

"Now I know why you were so coy about it."

"Was I?"

"You know you were. So—" Something had occurred to him while he was watching her with Marc and thinking about her world versus his world. "Are you testing me or something?"

"No." She swiveled to face him directly, looking alarmed.

"Okay. Because I am straight."

"Bryan, does that not go without saying? And it is true in more ways than one. You are direct about everything. To me it is refreshing."

"Uh-huh."

She rose to take the coffee from the assistant who knocked and brought it in. "*Merci.*"

The girl glanced at Bryan and closed the door behind her.

Odette fussed with the coffees and handed him his. They both drank, looking at each other over the rims of their cups.

He finished first and got up to toss the cup into the waste-basket. "Well, it's a beautiful morning and I'm sure you have work to do. I'm going to explore Paris."

"Do you want a driver?"

She put a hand on the phone and looked at him.

"No, I can walk. But thanks."

"As you wish." She paused for a beat. "Are you angry with me, Bryan?"

He shook his head. "No. I just got weirded out last night. Anyway, you have other things to worry about right now."

"What are you saying?" She sounded nervous and her boss lady confidence seemed to have dissolved. She really did have a lot on her plate.

"Look, I'm staying in Paris for the time being. And I'll help you with this, uh, situation if I can."

"Thank you."

Was she going to cry? Christ, he hoped not. "Let's just keep this light, okay? Things are happening a little too fast for me."

"Yes. I can do light." She gave him the kind of hopeful look that sent chills up his spine. A lot of men would have jumped at the chance to bed her, then use her. He was up for the first part, but not the second.

They were just too goddamn different was what it came down to. And yet, looking at her, he thought she was fucking perfect, funny clothes and all. Marc was a great guy, and so were some of the other people he'd met during a dizzying few days. But some of the others—a mean model he could name and the ambitious assistant who'd betrayed Odette—weren't. She didn't seem to care all that much. He wasn't sure what mattered to her, and he was feeling more and more like he was looking in through a window at a glittering party he hadn't really been invited to.

Yeah, the winning raffle ticket had opened the door and he'd found himself inside a freaky, glamorous world. He'd been open-mouthed when he found out by accident that she was one of its anointed queens.

But she hadn't told him that.

He'd come up with a flattering interpretation of the fact, like a giant fucking idiot.

"Can we talk later?" There was a trace of sadness in her tone, like she knew, just knew, he was having second thoughts.

"Sure." He had to say yes. That beseeching look in her eyes—he told himself not to kick her when she was down.

He nodded to the doorman who let him out of her atelier and thrust his hands in his pockets. First things first—he needed an internet café.

He could have checked his e-mail in her office, but he had to keep a little distance if he was going to keep his sanity.

The street had very few people on it, but the spring air was pleasantly moist and smelled kind of new and green. The freshly planted flower boxes on wrought iron balconies held pansies that trembled in the breeze, and tendrils of ivy reached down, softening the facades of the fine old houses.

Being outdoors cheered him up. He walked on aimlessly, until he got to a busier street, lined with cafés. A white-aproned waiter was lugging out chairs and setting them up at small marble tables, and there were quite a few customers having coffee already.

Overcoat-wearing old geezers reading newspapers. Chic women with dogs at their expensively shod feet. A couple of scruffy students in sandals and sweaters. Some of the best things about Paris were free to all. It was a great city, when all was said and done.

Bryan sighed and kept on going to where he'd spotted a sign for an internet joint up ahead.

He cupped a hand over his eyes and peered in through the glass door. The young proprietor waved him in and Bryan pushed the door open. He ordered a breakfast sandwich, needing a little fortification before he checked in with the real world and the guy nuked it for him.

Bryan took a seat at a monitor and pulled up his e-mail account with the hand that wasn't holding the wrapped sandwich.

One from his mother. He opened it right away.

How are you?

Three little words that he had to answer or he'd be in big trouble. His mom would send the Royal Californian Mounted Police on a global quest to find his ass if he didn't.

He took a bite of the sandwich and thought about what to say.

Still in Paris. Beautiful. Wish you could see it.

He looked through his previous e-mails and sent her the link to the article about him in *Bonjour Paris,* adding his own version of the event. Then he debated telling her about Odette.

Nuh-uh. Not yet.

He tapped out a couple of paragraphs about where he'd wandered in the city, leaving in the misspellings so she wouldn't think he was cribbing it from a travel guide and wrapped up with a few lines about his hiking trip in Alsace.

The fashion part would thrill her—she'd forward all that to her friends.

Okay. He was done. He added a *love ya* and clicked Send.

Bryan scrolled through the rest, picking up on a couple of .edu endings right away and opening those up.

Thank you for your interest in . . .

Yeah. He was still under consideration. Hurry up and wait some more, dude, was what they were basically saying.

He signed out, stuffing the last bite of his sandwich in his mouth and brushing the crumbs off his hands. A tall, brawny man walked by the window and glanced at him, then stopped in his tracks. Bryan smiled and got up to go, slam-dunking the crumpled paper from the sandwich on the way.

"Achille! What are you doing here?" He looked down and saw the Chihuahua pull on his thin leash, then sit down.

"Shopping. He won't walk more than a few steps and I cannot carry him," Achille said. He lifted his hands, which held bags bulging with his purchases, and lifted the little dog along with them. Jimmy gave an exasperated yap. "I should have left him at home."

Bryan reached for the leash. "I don't really have anything else to do. Leave him with me."

"Are you sure? Do you not have a headache after last night?"

"Gone."

Achille sighed as he looked at the dog. "He may give you another one. Sometimes I think we should send him to obedience training."

"This little guy? What's the point?"

Jimmy blinked his eyes, as if he was glad *someone* understood.

"All right then," Achille said. "Jimmy, be good. See you later, Bryan."

"Glad to help."

He looked at the dog, happy to have companionship on a day that had started off lousy, but was slowly improving. Then he realized that he couldn't sightsee with Jimmy on a leash.

Not a problem. Just walking around was fun, and Paris was full of parks. He would let Jimmy run free when they got to one where that was okay.

He gave a tug on the leash. Jimmy kept his skinny butt firmly planted on the pavement.

Bryan didn't feel like arguing. He scooped the dog up and tucked him in his jacket, his big-for-a-little-dog head hanging out. "How's that?"

Jimmy blinked blissfully.

Bryan walked on, heading back toward the first café he'd

passed, using it as a landmark. He wanted to buy a map at a kiosk and figure out which way to go next.

The wrought iron chairs were filled now, and the mix was a little different. More laptops, less lingering. A woman sitting at one looked at him over the screen, like a beauty of yesterday looking over a fan.

Nice eyes.

He realized that he'd seen them before. "Marie?"

"I thought it was you." Marie Arelquin stood up, laughing, and shook hands. "How have you been, Bryan?"

"Fine. I've been having a great time."

"Who is this?" She patted the Chihuahua's bony head.

"His name is Jimmy. He belongs to a friend."

She pulled up a chair for him. "Please, sit down."

"Aren't you working?"

Marie smiled. "Pretending to work, like half of Paris." She tapped a couple of keys and shut down the laptop, slipping it into its padded case.

"Okay then." He looked down. "Jimmy, lay low."

"It is all right to have a dog in a café. Sometimes even in a restaurant."

"Did you hear that?" he said to his jacket. The dog had curled up and was closing his eyes. "Aww. He's asleep."

"Good girl bait, a dog like that," Marie said mischievously.

Bryan shook his head. "I'm not looking for trouble."

"You mean Odette Gaillard isn't?"

He blushed a little. "You know about that?"

"Only that you two left the show together and she didn't take a bow. You must be having a very good time."

Bryan hemmed and hawed, and decided to act like he was famous and not confirm or deny anything. "She's really interesting. I didn't know you knew her—outside of professionally, I mean."

"We went to school together."

"Really." He found that reassuring. Marie Arelquin seemed totally normal. Even conservative. Her chic suit and the scarf neatly tied at the neck made her look older than Odette, though.

"She was not a very good student, but very bright, of course. She liked to have fun. Always in the director's office for one infraction or another, usually of the dress code. She made her own clothes, you know."

"I can imagine."

"She has always had a style that is all her own," Marie said warmly.

"I like it. The show was great. Never saw anything like it."

Marie folded her arms on the marble table and leaned forward a little. "So how much longer are you staying? And where are you staying?"

"Oh, a few weeks maybe. I'm crashing on a friend's couch."

"Is that the friend who Jimmy belongs to?"

"Yeah." He looked down into his jacket. "Still asleep."

He chatted with Marie for a while longer, enjoying the easygoing mood of a morning in Paris. The tense, sometimes frenzied vibe of Odette's business seemed far away. The city had a laid-back aspect. You just had to find it.

Odette was nowhere to be found when Bryan got back to the atelier. Marc caught up with him while he was walking around looking for her.

"There you are," Marc said. "Delphine said you'd come back. You've been gone for hours."

"Yeah, I went for a walk, got to talking, wandered around. Where's Odette?"

"In a fitting. Strict security. After what happened—"

"No need to explain," Bryan said.

Marc looked him over, noticing the bulge in his zipped jacket. "You look pregnant. Really, Bryan. Your clothes—"

"That would be your dog," Bryan interrupted him. He lowered the zipper carefully and pulled on the jacket so Marc could look in.

"*Zut!* Look how happy he is!" Marc gave Bryan a slap on the back. "You are so nurturing, you make me nauseous."

"Tough."

The dog gave Marc a bleary look and settled back down.

"Do you want to attend the fitting?" the assistant asked.

"Am I allowed?"

"Odette specifically said to ask you to come in."

Bryan shot him a doubtful glance. "Don't her clients mind having men in the room?"

"They assume we are all homosexual."

"Uh, well, I mind. Even Grischenka got me hot. For a little while. It just doesn't seem right. No, I'll wait."

Marc shrugged. "Suit yourself." He steered Bryan to an empty office not too far from the several rooms where fittings were done. "See you later. Don't let Jimmy pee on the carpet when he wakes up."

"Hell, no. I'm in charge, not him."

"Hah. Just you wait."

Bryan settled back in the swivel chair. It felt pretty good to sit down after a long walk on old streets. He'd covered some distance after leaving Marie Arelquin at the café.

Jimmy poked out his head to be petted and Bryan obliged him.

It wasn't long before something disturbed their peace. He could hear female voices that he figured were coming from the fitting rooms. Odette's was one. Soothing. And there were a couple of others. Fluttery.

And another one that rose over all the rest. Strident. Pissed-off. And weirdly familiar.

Bryan heard a door get yanked open and then bang shut behind someone angry. The sound of high heels, muted by the thick carpet they stabbed, was next.

"I look fat!" a woman shrieked. A blonde bombshell who'd been strapped and pinned into a barely-there bondage dress stalked past his door. "Really fat!"

Odette and several assistants came after her.

"Madame Krissie, please," said an anxious girl.

"Let her howl," Odette said. "She needs to."

Krissie? Even from the back, Bryan thought Odette's client looked familiar. No wonder he'd recognized the voice. Krissie Howard was the lead singer for Chaos. And she sure as hell didn't look fat.

This was a fitting he wanted to see. It was amazing how quickly certain scruples could be set aside.

He got up and looked down the hall. Krissie had gotten as far as she could without actually blasting through a wall cartoon-style. She was pounding on it instead, throwing a spectacular tantrum.

Odette stood to one side, her arms folded over her chest, her assistants standing behind her. They clutched scraps of black material and scissors.

"You have to fix this," Krissie snarled. "Now."

"Of course," Odette said patiently. "If you will please come with me." She extended a hand as if she hadn't heard one word of Krissie's ranting and raving.

Krissie tugged the dress down over her thighs. "I'm supposed to look wicked. Not pudgy."

"We can do wicked," Odette said soothingly.

The rock star tossed her bleached, crimped locks and condescended to be led back. Bryan stepped inside the door frame, hoping she wouldn't take a random swing at him.

But she made Odette stop.

"Oh my gawwwwd, look at the dog," she said. "I love dogs! Is he yours? Can I pet him?"

To his credit, Jimmy didn't shrink away. He was turning out to be tougher than Bryan expected.

Bryan felt a little tingle in his cock when Krissie bent over and cooed at the Chihuahua. A hot, sweaty smell emanated from her that was almost rank. Jimmy sniffed at her cleavage with interest.

Wrong species, little guy, Bryan thought with amusement. Even if she is a bitch. "Sure. Go ahead," was what he said.

He glanced at Odette, whose lips were pressed together. Her assistants were looking curiously at the dog.

Marie had been right. Jimmy was great girl bait. He got a hand around the dog's warm body and lifted him out of his jacket. "Say hi to everybody, Jimmy."

The dog's little legs danced in midair as he gave random licks to whoever touched him first.

"Can I hold him?" Krissie asked.

"Ah—okay." Despite his diminutive size, he was a man's dog. Bryan wasn't sure if Jimmy would take to someone as screechy as Krissie.

She let him curl up on her nearly bare bosom and the dog shot Bryan a *fooled-ya* look.

"You can come with us," the rock star said to Bryan. "I don't want him to miss his daddy."

Marc came around a corner, probably because he'd heard the commotion, and made a gagging face for Bryan and Odette's benefit without the star or the assistants seeing him. "*Oui,* Krissie," he said when he got closer. "Whatever you like. Bryan, come along."

He tagged after the group, ignoring a glare from Odette.

So she could be jealous. She wasn't so totally sophisticated that nothing really mattered to her. He was fine with that.

With the dog riding on her bosom, Krissie walked more gently. She cooed to Jimmy as Odette dropped behind to talk to Bryan, drawing to one side and letting her assistants return with Marc and the rock star to the fitting rooms.

"What do you think you're doing?"

"Nothing," he said blandly. "I was just standing there with Marc's dog. Now she's happy."

"I am not."

Bryan touched a hand to her lower back, as if he was guiding her down the hallway. What he was really doing was assessing her. In his experience, women often said one thing and felt another. He was getting a melty vibe from her, like she wasn't really mad.

"Leave early. We can both be happy," he said.

"What's got into you?"

Bryan shrugged. He was actually glad to be relieved of the dog, although he'd enjoyed the attention he got with him. "I had a great walk. Mellowed me out."

"You weren't so very mellow when you left this morning."

"No, I wasn't. I had a hangover and—"

"You said things were happening too fast for you. *Tant pis.*"

He knew what that meant. Tough luck. But her bravado didn't match the look he'd seen in her eyes this morning. "Hey, settle down." He ran a hand down her spine and got that melty vibe again. "I got some fresh air, played in the park. I'm an outdoors guy, remember?"

She nodded.

"A hothouse like this"—he gestured at the striking photos of ultra-glam models and stars as they passed them on the walls—"is not my natural environment. But here I am."

"*Bien.* You are a good sport. Will you come in for Krissie's fitting? She is a world-class bitch but I believe she likes you."

"Anything for fashion." He dropped a kiss on Odette's hair, feeling a little guilty about the way he was playing her.

The star was in the middle of the fitting room as they entered, her arms above her head, standing on a low box. Marc had his little dog back, and Jimmy's pop-eyes were taking in the scene.

Wide bands of black stretchy material were being pinned around Krissie by two dressmaking assistants.

"Squeeze me!" Krissie said loudly. "I love the feeling!"

"Does it help you make the high notes?" Marc said. "Justine, pull tighter."

Krissie's big breasts bulged over the top part. "Oo, yes," she giggled, looking down. "Strap those puppies *down.*"

Justine moved the bands of material so that the maximum amount of skin elsewhere was visible.

"Please look in the mirror, Madame Howard," she said.

Krissie jumped down from her six-inch pedestal and strutted over, hands on her swinging hips. She jumped up and down, making her boobs jiggle. "More bounce to the ounce. My man fans will go wild."

"No doubt," Marc said icily. "Odette, what do you think?"

Odette looked her client over. "Should we reveal more of her bottom?"

Bryan wished he could think of something useful to do besides just look on. Say, pick lint off the carpet with tweezers. Something that would demand his close and undivided attention.

Odette went over to Krissie and began to tug at the bands of material, pulling them down. Her ass cleavage was revealed and it was as spectacular as the front. "*Comme ça,*" Odette said with satisfaction, turning to the two men. "What do you think?"

"It balances the balcony," Marc said.

Bryan didn't say anything.

Krissie pirouetted in front of the mirror, turning to get a rear view. A mischievous look came into her eyes, and she turned again, stepping toward Bryan.

She faced him and then turned her ass toward him, bending over with her hands on her knees. Then she thrust backward against his crotch before he could move and pressed her soft ass firmly into him. He gasped but got erect in less than three seconds.

He couldn't step away because she was sure to fall if he did.

She felt his hard-on. She positioned her behind just right, kept his rod in between her barely-wrapped cheeks, and slid over it. Little squats. Effective toners for her hips, thighs, and buttocks. Killer move on his trapped dick.

"Road test," she announced. "Is that working for you, Dog Daddy?"

He caught Odette's glare and returned it with a look of helplessness mingled with, he was sure, inadvertent lust.

Getting a rub from a plump set of very feminine ass cheeks caused an inevitable biological reaction that had everything to do with the law of evolution. Krissie's slow, voluptuous movement would ensure the transmission of his DNA to future generations.

Meaning he was about to come in his pants.

Then Marc pretended to drop the dog, catching Jimmy in midair just as Krissie straightened up.

Bryan shot him a grateful look. He took Krissie by the hips and lifted her forward. If he pushed, she'd topple over.

"Gotcha!" A man with a graying, limp ponytail and sunglasses breezed in, his cell phone held out in take-a-picture position. "Krissie, you're too much. Who's your latest victim?"

"Delete that, Max." She laughed as she straightened. "I really don't know."

"Sure looked like you knew him real well."

She yawned. "Nah. I was just fooling around."

Bryan wasn't sure if the photo had been deleted from the phone or not. The man was fiddling with the buttons and frowning at the tiny screen.

"You took that off, right?" Bryan said, trying to keep his voice friendly.

"Sure, sure." The limp ponytail flipped in Bryan's face as the man turned around to greet a lot of other people who actually did seem to know Krissie real well. They barged into the room, and Marc introduced Bryan to her manager, her publicist, her hairdresser, her agent, the band's manager, and three or four losers, male and female, who fell into the broader category of entourage. There was no way he was going to remember all those names. But he had to hand it to Marc for being able to.

"Whaddya think?" Krissie modeled the banded dress, bending over, flipping her hair around, wiggling her ass. "Am I a cheap tramp or what?"

"Cheap from Oh! Oh! Odette costs big bucks," someone said. "But you're worth it."

"You're a fucking riot," Krissie retorted. "I wanna know if this will work on stage."

"You can make anything work, baby girl," her manager said, leering at her.

She stepped and strutted, loving that she was the center of attention. Then she stopped in front of the mirror, loving her reflection. She ran a hand seductively up and down her bare thighs. "It'll do."

Bryan looked at Odette, who didn't quite meet his glance.

"This design is totally exclusive, right?" Krissie asked Odette.

"It was made for you and on you," Odette said. "Of course it is exclusive."

"Mine, mine, mine?"

Odette tipped her head to one side and folded her arms over her chest. "Not forever. It will be photographed and copied after you appear on stage."

"But I'd better be the only tramp in it when I step out in front of the band. Speaking of those guys, did anyone wake them up yet?"

"I took a peeky-weeky in the suite. Your bass player's still conked out," her agent said. "And ya know, he snores better than he plays."

"Was there anyone else with him?" Krissie wanted to know.

"Three or four girls, sleeping in a heap. And the drummer. He could be dead. He was underneath."

"Get another one in time for the show."

The band manager guffawed. "Better hope you don't have to. Hey, I checked in on Guitar Joe and the new sax man. They were awake. They were fighting over the pot supply."

"What a bunch of crazy fucks. I hate them all," Krissie said, chewing thoughtfully on a lock of her bleached hair. "Can't I just go solo?"

"No, baby," her agent crooned. "We need those guys to drown you out and there isn't time to rehearse a new bunch of crazy fucks. We talked about this, Krissie. Your voice is studio quality. Stage singing could strain it and that's not what we want. We want to use our lips, not our throat. Synch or swim."

"I guess you're right." Krissie blew out a sigh and pouted. "Tell Joe and Kareem to knock it off, though. I don't like fighting. Take the pot away."

"I can't do that. They just bought it."

"If I may interrupt," Odette said. "We should resume the fitting."

Krissie gave a huge groan. "Fuck it. I'm sick of being stuck with pins. I want to get out of here."

"Sure, sure," the ponytailed guy said soothingly. "We all do."

"But we just got here," said someone from the entourage. "Can't we, like, look around?"

"No," Odette said firmly.

"Score some freebies?"

She motioned over an assistant. "Take them down to the sample room and see what there is that they can have."

"We want those teeny shopping bags to put the goodies in," a girl whined. "Like, for proof that we were here."

Not caring who was watching her, Krissie began to peel off the stretchy bands. Her bare breasts popped out first and she was working on sliding the rest down over her hips, until Ponytail Man stopped her with a tap on the shoulder.

"Not here, Krissie. Save it for the ones you love: your fans."

"Yeah, right," she grumbled. "Fuck my fucking fans. Okay, everybody out."

The people who'd come into the room were guided to the door by the assistant who'd been dragooned into taking them to the sample room. She followed them into the hall and closed the door behind herself.

Krissie took the opportunity to strip off the rest of the dress-in-progress and handed it nonchalantly to Odette. Bryan looked studiously at the floor as the star slid on breathtakingly tight jeans and a microscopic T-shirt.

Next up were boots, a leather jacket, sunglasses, and a swaggeringly bad attitude that was put on like an accessory.

She hoisted a gigantic Louis Vuitton satchel over her shoulder. "Okay. Thanks, Odette. Fun fooling around with you, dude," she said to Bryan.

He nodded politely, and Krissie sashayed out, looking for her tribe.

"I am glad that's over," Odette said. "But she is a walking advertisement for my edge designs. I have to keep her happy."

"You did well, Odette," Marc said, stroking Jimmy before

he put the dog down and let him run around the fitting room. "I think she liked the dress. The bondage look is still hot and Krissie wears it well."

"She does," Odette sighed. "That girl is hard to handle. I need to get out of here myself. Bryan, what's it like out?"

He looked at her wan face and felt a little guilty. "Nice. Really nice. Want to take a break and wander around for a while?"

She brightened up immediately. "Yes. Marc, I am leaving you in charge." She thrust the handful of material that had gone into Krissie's exclusive dress at him. "Mind the pins. Don't misplace it."

Marc took the handful of material and stuffed it into a manila envelope. He wrote *Krissie Chaos* on it and sealed the envelope. "I will put it into the safe in your office."

"Good," Odette said absently. "Let's go. I need fresh air and sunshine."

"Go fool around," Marc said sternly. "You must. The Jardin des Plantes is just the place."

10

They strolled hand in hand down a walkway lined with tall old trees just leafing out.

"Such a tender green," Odette murmured. "I love the new-ness of it."

"You could design a leaf bra," Bryan said. "Like the flower-petal one. With a matching thong. All you would need is one leaf for the front."

"Hmm. Not a bad idea, Bryan."

"Feel free to steal it."

Odette groaned. "Oh, do not even say that word. Just think-ing about the flower fiasco gives me a headache. I am sure my beautiful design is on millions of bodies by now. Bah."

"Mmm. Millions of bare-naked women covered in flower petals. Sounds good to me."

Odette snorted. "You didn't move away from Krissie's, I noticed."

"I couldn't," Bryan protested. "I didn't want to knock the queen of alt-rock flat on her face."

"It would do her good."

But she didn't seem to really care about it, and dropped the subject. "I think perhaps I will not go back to the atelier today."

"All right with me."

"And how do you like living with Mark and Achille?"

"They're very nice and very domestic."

"Yes, I would agree. But will you come home with me tonight?"

"Sure."

He couldn't think of one good reason to say no.

They had come to an area with a more landscaped look and he noticed a sign for the museum of natural history in the near distance. "I didn't know this was here. How cool is that? Back in California I was talking online to a guy who maintains their shell collection—he was very helpful."

"Do you want to go in?"

He shook his head. "Seems like a shame to waste the sunshine."

Odette waved her hand at the sky. "I will call up the clouds."

He laughed at her gesture. "Why?'

"So that we can do something you want to do. I feel that I am dragging you into my crazy life."

"I enjoy it," he said, giving her a light kiss. "And I can take care of myself." He looked again at the museum.

"You do want to go in. Come," she said, pulling at his hand. "You can meet your friend, maybe. And we can look at shells. I might find inspiration, and there is plenty of day left."

"All right." He really didn't need persuading.

As they got closer, he looked at the big exhibition banner waving over the entrance. A luminous squid was splashed upon it.

"*Les Abysses*." Odette read the sign and looked pleased. "There you are. The ocean awaits you, right in the middle of Paris."

"I can't say no."

They paid the admission and entered, blinking in the cool semi-darkness inside. Odette moved from one display to another, oohing and ahhing over the oddities and monsters of the deep.

"Help me out here," he said, trying to read an explanatory plaque that was all in French.

"*Plongez dans les abysses!*" she began in a dramatic voice, "*et—*"

He gave her butt a friendly squeeze. "I'd rather *plonge* into you."

"Shut up." She went on reading. "*Milieux et peuplements aquatiques . . .* oh, it goes on and on." She had perked up, fired by a schoolgirlish curiosity. "Never mind the blah-blah. What is in here? Is this where to begin, in the shallow water?"

Bryan looked into the tank and glanced at another explanatory plaque that would take him forever to read. "Oysters. Not very exciting. Except to other oysters."

"Look, the big one is on top of the small one. Are they mating?"

"Not exactly. Oysters don't do it like that—"

She wasn't listening. "Love among the mollusks," she sighed happily. "They too have romantic feelings. Who knew?"

He didn't feel like disillusioning her, and they moved on.

"*Quel horreur!*" she exclaimed, looking at a filament-sprouting, goggle-eyed, needle-toothed fish, the star of an undersea film that appeared at the touch of a button. The fish swallowed everything that floated by and then retreated to its lair, looking gloomy.

"Not so inspiring, huh?" Bryan grinned.

"No, it is not."

They moved through several galleries, and doubled back to

the shells. "Ah, such colors," she sighed appreciatively in front of a gorgeous display. "And the shapes—very sexual."

He came up behind her and rested his chin on the top of her head, circling his arms around her waist. She relaxed and leaned back against him as he named the ones he was familiar with.

"You know so many. I am impressed."

"Don't be. There's a lot here I've never seen. This is an out-standing collection."

"*C'est plus beau.*"

"It sure is." He didn't mind her appreciating it for purely aesthetic reasons.

"Is your friend around here, Bryan?"

"No, I don't think so. He's not really a friend, just someone who helped me with research. He's probably in the back offices or someplace like that, organizing specimen cases."

"Playing with beautiful shells. What a wonderful job."

Bryan chuckled. "It's work, like anything else."

"And I am having a very good time, running away from mine." She looked up at him and in another second they got wrapped up in a kiss that went on for a while. There weren't very many visitors over this way, so there weren't kids staring when they came up for air.

"Ah," she sighed. "I wish we could hop on a plane and go collect our own on a beach far away."

"Yeah, that'd be nice," he said absently, smoothing back her hair and giving her a few more kisses on her cheek.

"Would you really go?"

"Huh?"

"We could take a long weekend in Martinique. Or St. Barts. Or Dominica. Such a pretty island and not overcrowded."

"Well, now. I have to go home eventually."

"It was just a thought," she said lightly.

Bryan had a feeling she wanted him to respond with more enthusiasm. But he wasn't ready to step into the whirlwind of her life, as amazing as it was.

"Tell you what," he said. "I'll treat you to something even better when we get to your house. You won't have to pack. You won't even have to leave your bed."

"I can already imagine it," she said. "Damask roses, scented candles . . . "

She leaned over and lit the last of five pillar candles, arranged in a circle around a vase of full-blown hothouse roses. Their mingled scents were subtle, wafting through the room on the slight breeze coming in the open window.

The evening was warm and he'd stripped down to jeans soon enough. Just padding around on Odette's thick carpets was a pleasure. They'd bought the roses on the way, and eaten at a bistro, which was a good thing, because there wasn't much in the fridge besides several bottles of the world's most expensive champagne in case they got thirsty.

He felt very much at home.

And Odette Gaillard had one hell of a home. He'd gotten a better look at the art on the walls and the combination of designer furniture and flea market finds. She really had a great eye—no surprise there.

Yeah, her place beat his place all to hell.

He ran a hand over the armrest of the clear Lucite armchair with the roses embedded in it. Not the kind of thing you'd stretch out in at the end of the day, but it was growing on him.

Bryan decided against sitting in it. Standing and watching her light the candles in that sex goddess outfit gave his erection more room to lengthen.

She was in nothing but black lace, a retro outfit from the

1950s that was doing nice things for his dick. The bra cups were seamed to a provocative point and the lace panties were lined with satin for modesty's sake.

There was something about the incredibly retro idea of modesty itself that turned him on to the max.

He wanted to take his sweet time about getting her naked. Revealing every inch of Odette's naked beauty nice and slow. Just looking at her thighs above the tops of her stockings was making him hot.

The garters themselves were a trip, their nipple-like bumps pressed through metal clasps and snapped into gossamer silk. She let him watch her put her stockings on, but she hadn't let him touch her.

And oh my God, the high heels she had on.

Spiked. Very low cut. Plenty o' toe cleavage. They did fantastic things for her legs. Shoes for shoe-worshippers. Bryan didn't classify himself as one, but he understood that heels like that were made to be worn in bed.

He wasn't sure where to start.

Odette straightened and blew out the match. Her lips pouted, red and slick.

Uh-huh. The head of his cock would fit nicely into that plump circle of moist flesh.

He let his eyes run all over her when she turned around.

Unbelievable.

How come the best get-your-freak-on underwear was from the 1950s, back when women weren't supposed to enjoy sex? Temptation had to have been much more . . . tempting once upon a time.

"What are you thinking?"

The ultimate female question. At the moment, he didn't feel like he had to answer. Words weren't enough, anyway.

Action. He could hear the word in his head like he was directing a movie.

But this was for real.

"I'm thinking about what I want to do to you first. I can't make up my mind."

She took the initiative, strolling in front of him with her hands on her hips, and staying just out of reach. When she reached the clear armchair, she sat in it, then spread her legs apart.

Her pose was wanton but she managed to make it elegant.

There was no seeing through those panties. As he watched, her forefinger disappeared under them and she closed her eyes, masturbating delicately as if he wasn't there at all.

Her private pleasure, on public display for an audience of one, but not her private parts. Interesting.

She used her other hand to press and rub the silk-lined lace against her pussy. Her mouth formed that plump, slick pout again and she pulled her finger out of her panties to stick in her mouth and suck.

Man. Watching this was heaven.

Odette opened her eyes and gave him a dreamy look as she pulled her wet finger out. Then she spread her legs even wider and arched her back, thrusting her hips forward. She gave her stimulated pussy a vigorous spanking, giving a little cry with each blow, punishing it sensually.

Bryan rubbed himself through his jeans, watching what she was doing very intently.

"Stand up," he said at last.

She did, stretching a little, still elegant, playing a sophisticated slut. Odette went over to her mirror, wiping away most of the lipstick. Preparing for . . . him. Or so he hoped. Her lips looked swollen, tinged with scarlet. The pout was the same, but there was no lipstick left to smear on his cock or his face. Excellent.

She came back, swinging her hips as only a woman in really high heels could, and stood in front of him, her hands on her hips. There was something brazen in her stance. She looked tougher than usual but he liked it.

He slid his hand between the tops of her thighs, stroking the silken skin there until she purred under her breath. Then he tested the lined lace of the panties. Nice and wet.

Odette took his head in her hands and kissed him feverishly. Little by little, she moved down, pressing hot kisses to his neck, bare chest, against his fly, and ended up on the floor.

She got on all fours, high heels still on. Her ass was cupped and firmly held by the gorgeous panties, and her breasts fell forward into the pointed cups of the bra, almost overflowing them.

He walked around her, his eyes devouring the sight of her in this submissive position.

Then he stood over her, straddling her so that he faced her ass. He bent down and reached into her panties, roughly squeezing the confined flesh and stimulating her.

He pulled his hands out, having noticed an interesting feature of the panties: a nearly invisible zipper running down the back seam.

Easy to undo. She was a few seconds away from bare-bottom discipline and she seemed to know it. He brought his legs closer to her body, pressing them against her waist and felt her tremble.

Odette was into this.

He reached down and unzipped her panties. The round globes of her ass bore the imprint of the silk seams. The thin red marks in the white softness of her skin excited him.

"You want a spanking, don't you?"

"*Oui, m'sieu.* I need one. I crave your firm hand."

So he was her m'sieu. A man with no name. And she was

anonymous, her face unseen, but the most vulnerable parts of her on full display.

Bryan, forgetting about everything but what she'd just said, gave her a good one. His hand stung when he was done, the palm red as her bottom.

Odette had tried to stay still, but he was into it, and did the honors a little more forcefully. The way she shook all over when his hand came down was something he found incredibly exciting.

Bryan straightened up and walked over her, then turned around for the full picture, sitting down in the armchair she'd sat in only minutes ago, masturbating while he watched.

No matter what position she was in, he loved looking his fill. Right now, her panties unzipped in back, her dirty-girl show of her bare buttocks, the glowing color his hands had left on them, the stockings and high heels she still had on—fuck. Better than beautiful.

11

_____

Waking up after a night like that, he was unfuckingbelievably relaxed.

And so was she.

Sound asleep, Odette lay in his arms, her lips just touching his right nipple, her even breathing making his chest feel warm.

He turned his head carefully, keeping his body still so as not to wake her, and looked toward the windows. The shutters were closed, but not all the way. The sky of Paris was a pearl gray.

He guessed it was, oh, a little after six o'clock in the morning. Bryan sighed with contentment. He had done his manly duty by her and gotten maximum pleasure out of it.

What a woman. He was going to dream about her in black lace for the rest of his life.

The thought made his heart beat faster. Hell. He looked down at her wonderful face and felt a flash of sudden sadness.

Deep as their sexual connection had been, he wasn't some kid who was going to mistake the way he'd been all shook up by her for love.

Romantic as the city of lights was, he still wasn't walking around in a movie and Paris wasn't a backdrop.

It was her home town. Not his, though. Bryan sighed and Odette stirred in her sleep.

"Sorry, angel," he murmured.

She moved off him and lay on her side, lost in a dream.

Of him?

He was vain enough to hope so. He even hoped that she wouldn't miss him when the day came—hell. He'd seen her use the little laptop in the kitchen that she kept plugged in to check e-mail and the weather widget. He had to check on the status of the plane ticket he'd put on hold.

And make coffee.

Figuring out what was going to happen next with him and Odette required serious quantities of caffeine.

Bryan eased his naked self out of the bed, trying to rise like he was levitating. He succeeded to some degree, because she still didn't stir. All right. Padding to the kitchen, he found the French press for coffee and got water boiling.

He dumped in several scoops of coffee. On second thought, he dumped in double that. Once done, the brew smelled heavenly and he poured it out into a big cup, pulling the little laptop on the counter toward him. The screen flickered to life when he did.

Raised not to snoop, he kept his eyes firmly fixed on the navigation bar and entered his Hotmail address.

Click and click and click. The airline's reservation advisory service hadn't sent him anything. So he was still in traveler's limbo, after canceling his flight home.

Bryan took a deep breath, not really wanting to check his bank balance. But he had to. He typed in the website and his code, and winced when he saw his balance.

That bad?

It was a good thing Marc had been nice enough to put him up, and Odette had insisted on going to inexpensive restaurants. He felt kinda like a charity case, but he would have been wildly fucking overdrawn if he hadn't been careful.

And now, ta da, he had $2.06 left in his account. Bryan was pretty sure that didn't add up to a whole euro, not at the current dismal rate of exchange.

He signed out of the site and sipped his coffee. If he was going to stay on, he would have to get some off-the-books job. For which he would have to ask for help from Odette.

Way to go, Bachman, he told himself. How to impress a rich chick.

"Bryan?"

Her sleepy voice called from the bedroom. There was longing in it, and a sweetness underneath that he knew he craved. She'd opened him up so much last night that he could think that way.

The last thing he wanted, though, was to *feel* that way.

"Coming, babe."

He poured another coffee for her and brought both with him back to the bedroom.

"There you are." She was propped on her elbow, looking totally hot, even with snarled hair.

"Here you go."

"*Merci.* You are very nice to get up and make it." She took a sip and grimaced. "It is very strong."

"Oh, yeah. Sorry about that. Want me to put some milk in it?"

"No, that is okay. I should get up." She put the cup on the nightstand and got up, walking around to find her robe.

The phone rang.

"Now who is that?" Odette glanced at the clock. "It is only six-forty-five."

"Don't answer it."

"No?" She gave him a worried look. "What if it is my mother? She usually calls me every Friday or I call her."

The persistent ringing made him think Odette might be right. It sounded determined and mommish somehow.

Odette picked up the receiver and he could hear someone say her name, followed by a lot of fast French. Her eyes widened.

"*Mon Dieu,*" she murmured. "*Oui, continuez.*"

Whoever it was gave her an earful. Odette's expression grew more and more concerned.

"What is it?" he whispered.

She shook her head and mouthed *shhh*. Five minutes later she hung up the phone. "Krissie's dress was copied."

"Oh, no."

She nodded ruefully. "It seems there are pictures of the knockoff all over the internet."

"That was fast."

"That is how it happens, Bryan."

He set aside the coffee he was holding. No loss. It really was pretty vile. "Now what?"

"That was my workroom manager, Fanny. I don't think you met her. Anyway, her daughter is a big fan of Chaos and was looking online for pictures of Krissie. And there she was in the dress."

Bryan remembered with a sinking heart that the agent had taken his picture with Krissie in the dress, and was too dumb to have figured out how to delete it. Talk about being in a compromising position. Bryan undoubtedly resembled a smirking pervert and for all the world to see.

"Was I, uh, in the picture?"

Odette only laughed. "That is the least of my worries right now. But I don't know. We can go see."

She found her robe and cinched the sash tightly, going ahead of him back to the kitchen. She pulled the laptop over to her—he was grateful that the screen had gone black, not wanting her to know that he'd used it or why. Odette googled two words: *Chaos* and *Krissie*.

"*Zut*," she said angrily. "Fanny was right. Look at that."

Bryan took a deep breath, possibly the deepest breath he'd ever taken. He prayed that the photo wasn't too revealing. Then he looked.

"Okay," he said. "Not so bad."

His head had been mercifully cut off. No one would ever know it was him. The agent had focused on Krissie's big, bouncy boobs. It was clear that she was grinding her behind against someone's jeans, but not whose.

Bryan let out his breath in a whoosh of relief. Holy fuck. Saved by incompetence.

Odette enlarged the photo, studying it carefully, and he looked again. His random thoughts were on Krissie now.

Easy to see why one person was born to be a rock star and not others. She hadn't looked that sexy in person. But bent over the way she was, her wide, full mouth open and her white teeth showing, she had it going on, even in a grainy, slightly out of focus cell phone photo.

"There is no way the dress could have been copied from that," Odette was saying. "Fanny said to look here..." The photo disappeared as she typed in other websites. "There it is!"

Bryan saw what he thought was the same dress, although he couldn't say he remembered it all that well.

"But isn't it just, like, black bands of material?"

"No. It is where the black bands were and that she has been

photographed in it that makes it worth copying. Chaos is at the top of the charts. Every female under twenty-five knows Krissie and they will want that very dress."

Bryan nodded. "And I guess it doesn't help that Krissie is a bitch."

"No." Odette's tone was curt. "She will be livid. I expect she will call. Her manager will refuse to pay. And I had to pay overtime to the assistants to come in that day."

"I get it. She thinks the world revolves around her."

Odette nodded, shutting down the laptop. Without saying another word, she got out a frying pan and the makings of breakfast, bashing and rattling her way through it.

But she slid the final result, a very fluffy omelette, onto his plate with automatic tenderness. "Eat," she said. "It is going to be a difficult day."

They convened in the workroom, a larger space than the individual fitting room.

"We are the first to arrive, I see," Odette said, looking around.

"Looks like."

He glanced around, seeing the familiar dressmaker's things: dummies, and sewing machines and, in the very middle of the room, an enormous table.

Odette went to a chest of very wide, long drawers and used a key to open the top one. "I will brief you before the others arrive."

"Okay. Sounds very James Bond."

She shrugged. "Fashion piracy is not violent. But we do lose millions."

"That must suck."

"Most of all for the people whose jobs are at stake." She took an enormous, spiral bound book out of the drawer and laid it on the table. It looked something like her ring binder, but a whole hell of a lot bigger.

"What's that?" he asked.

She flipped it open. "This is the master book. The *vendeuse* uses it to keep track of customer orders in every detail."

"And a *vendeuse* is—"

"In charge of each creation from start to finish."

He wanted to look through the pages, but he had a feeling he'd get his hand slapped.

"Every couturier loses money on individual creations. They are simply too expensive to make and there are only a few thousand women in the whole world who can afford it."

"So . . . " He really didn't want to say *so what*. But he was thinking it.

"It is the cachet of designing for someone as young and famous as a rock star like Krissie that is lucrative. And mass market versions of the design for her that we can license bring in tremendous amounts of money."

"Is it really that complicated to make designer underwear?"

Way to go. Ask her irritating questions. But Odette didn't snap at him.

"To be registered as a couture house, I have to make fifty new designs for each collection—meaning dresses. You didn't see those, just the underwear."

"Hey, I'm a guy. I noticed what was important to me."

She smiled a little ruefully. "We left early, that was all."

"Right. So you were saying—"

"And I have to show at least two collections a year, and I have to employ at least twenty people in my atelier. I have more than forty."

"Who sets all these rules?"

"The *Chambre Syndicale de La Couture*. It is done to protect the traditions of *haute couture*. And we get free advertising on state TV."

"Okay. Sounds reasonable."

Odette leafed through the book. "I am looking for Krissie's page. We have everyone in here under code names."

Bryan wasn't sure if he was supposed to look or not.

"Here she is." Odette looked up as other people entered, holding takeout cups of coffee and tea.

"Here who is?" Marc asked. He had a thick scarf wrapped around his neck.

"Krissie. I wanted to find out what stage her dress was at."

Sabine, the workroom manager, took off her coat as Marc glanced her way. "We had begun the muslin pattern," she said to Odette.

Bryan looked hopefully at Marc, who took him aside to clear up his obvious confusion. "I thought that dress was, like, a handful of ripped stuff," he whispered.

"No, not once Odette draped and styled it on Krissie. From it, a pattern would be made. They had started it but not, apparently, finished it."

"Didn't you put the original in Odette's safe?"

Marc nodded. "I took it out so work could begin. The original is laid *mis à plat*—flat on the worktable—and the muslin pattern is taken directly from it. It is skilled work, even for such an eccentric design as Krissie's dress."

Odette had overheard and she took it upon herself to explain more to Bryan. "As flimsy as it looked, it had to last through a performance. And Krissie is a wild woman on stage. We would have made her several, each sewn by hand."

"Got it."

She turned away, becoming involved in a murmured conversation with Fanny and Sabine.

"The book is our record of who, what, and when," Marc

went on. "That way an actress on the red carpet will not see her mirror image, and the wife of a rich man will not see her husband's mistress in the same dress. We try to avert such disasters."

"Right." He was feeling more like a fish out of water every minute. The crunchy granola crowd he ran with had no clue that clothes did anything more than keep the rain out and the warmth in.

A few more people filed in and the meeting began in earnest.

"All right," Odette said. "As most of you know, some of my designs have been stolen—the flower ones first. We have begun an investigation."

Bryan wondered if she trusted everyone here enough to tell them that. She must. These were her older employees, except for Marc. Lucie, of course, had not been invited.

She wouldn't have had a chance to boost the dress design.

"But now that Krissie's dress has been stolen too, we must face the fact that there is a serious lapse in our security. For now—" she hesitated "we will have to close the atelier down. None of you are suspects."

But the dismay on their faces was clear. A few glanced suspiciously at Bryan.

"A computer expert will be going through the hard drives of the assistants' computers later. None of you work with computers, so that is another reason I have to trust you."

Her voice wavered and Bryan knew she was about to cry. He made a move to go to her, but Marc's hand on his arm stopped him.

"And for now, that is all I have to say."

Fanny, the *vendeuse*, stepped forward. "Madame Gaillard, if I may look through the book with you . . . "

"Please do," Odette said.

The older woman set the half glasses on a chain around her

neck on her nose. She was dressed in a smock, impeccably cut, severe but chic.

Bryan looked around at the serious faces. The rag trade was a lot more complicated than he'd ever imagined. Whatever. He'd help her if he could.

"Follow me," Odette said to Bryan when the workroom staff had gone home. "I will need moral support when I call Krissie's manager."

"Which one was he? The guy with the ponytail was her agent and then there was the band manager—I know he's different—"

Odette gave a short laugh. "I barely remember them all myself. I am glad that I do not have to see his face when he yells at me."

"If they want an exclusive, they shouldn't post cell phone pictures on the Chaos website."

She managed a faint smile. "Would you like to tell them that?"

"I will if you want me too."

"*Merci*, Sir Galahad."

He sat with her through several phone calls to different outraged people. He could've punched a few of the pigs on her behalf, no problem.

She hung up on the last one and said terrible things in French about him under her breath. Then she looked at him, tapping her pencil on the ring binder. "And now, the High Council meets."

"What? Who are they?"

"Women."

He held up his hands. "No boys allowed?"

"You are not a boy. And of course you may come."

Bryan rose and reached out a hand to her. She took it, getting to her feet. "Thank you."

"I've got to live up to the Galahad thing."

Odette gave him a worried look and a much too brief kiss. "So far, you are a natural."

The High Council turned out to be composed of two women—three, if you counted Odette.

There was Madame Arelquin, whom he had met before—but he'd just found out she was Odette's godmother. The old lady was dressed to the nines in a suit and a hat and gloves, which she held in one hand.

And Odette's mother, whom he hadn't met and hadn't been expecting to meet. He'd said a silent, drenched-in-irony thank-you to Odette for not telling him in advance.

Madame Gaillard had once been as beautiful as her daughter, if not as glamorous or as tall. Her hands showed that she'd worked with them for decades, but her roundness of body had kept her face looking much younger than her years.

Meeting even one of her parents under the circumstances was truly weird. But Madame Gaillard didn't seem to mind at all.

Odette tapped on the workroom table with a ruler. "Shall we begin?"

The two older women stopped chatting and looked her way.

"*Bien sûr*," Madame Arelquin said.

"Since you ran your own couture house, I wanted to know if this ever happened to you," Odette said. "The copying and stealing, I mean."

"Indeed it did. Long ago."

"And what did you do?"

Madame Arelquin looked at Madame Gaillard. "Your *maman* had just started working for me then. She was the one who told me that my designs had been copied—she had seen them at Bon Marché."

"What did you do?"

"Eventually we found the culprit," Madame Arelquin said. "We had him guillotined."

"Be serious," Odette's mother scolded her.

"I wanted to," Madame Arelquin replied. "Of course, there is very little that can be done. The man was sacked. The designs were worn by every shopgirl in Paris."

"Not a tragedy," Odette's mother replied.

"No," Madame Arelquin said. "But after that I was far more careful to hire only people I knew well. And no one was permitted to visit my atelier just to look around."

The old lady favored Bryan with a penetrating stare and he felt himself turn red.

If she was implying that he had anything to do with the theft—

"Odette invited me to visit," he said.

Madame Arelquin gave a faint sniff. "I see. Well, Odette, what I was going to say was that you should investigate those who are closest to you, and then the people who are closest to them. It will be only a few degrees of separation between you and the guilty."

"Why is that?"

"Because you are most likely to trust them. And where there is a great deal of money to be made, someone will take advantage of that trust."

"I hate to even think so," Odette said, dismayed.

"It is the way of the world."

"*Oui*," Odette's mother said, looking with concern at her daughter.

Madame Arelquin could not seem to stop looking at him, Bryan thought with annoyance. "With all due respect, Madame, I had nothing to do with it. I visited the atelier because I wanted to take a few pictures for my mother, who's a dressmaker."

Both old ladies were looking at him with a mixture of suspicion and sentimental interest.

"You did not mention that when we met at Odette's show," Madame Arelquin said at last.

"I didn't have a chance. There was a lot going on."

Madame gave a little cough into her hand. "It looked like the *Folies Bergère*. All those feathers and bare breasts—*alors*. Too much flesh."

"Now, now," Odette's mother chided. "It is not like it was in our day. Fashion is much more exciting."

"I suppose so," Madame Arelquin sighed. "But I miss the old days. Elegance! Restraint! Diana Vreeland frowning—how she could frown!"

"You never liked her," Odette's mother said. "You said she was a cow. A skinny cow."

"Hmph."

Odette put her head in her hands. "What should I do?"

"My dear girl, it seems to me that you are doing everything you can. Some would say that the bad publicity is a good thing, because it keeps your name in the news. And no one cares if a rock star's dress is stolen."

"Would you agree, Madame Arelquin?" Odette asked.

"No. Piracy is a terrible thing for our business and rock stars will be the death of it." She studied Bryan again. "But perhaps the young swashbuckler will take them on for you."

"If we can find them."

"Have you any leads?" Odette's mother asked her daughter.

"The computer expert manipulated a digital photo and found an address on a piece of paper in a purse belonging to one of my assistants."

"Do not keep us in suspense. Whose address was it?"

"King Khong."

Madame Arelquin's thin, arched eyebrows rose to her hair-

213

line. "I remember that odd name. My daughter mentioned it. He is notorious."

"Did he not steal from you before, Odette?" her mother asked.

"Yes, he did."

"Interpol can never seem to catch such thieves," Madame Arelquin said. "They pop up all over the world. When one sweatshop is closed down, another one opens somewhere else."

"The address is in New York."

Madame Arelquin scowled. "There, you see, that is what they do. I remember Marie saying that he was in China."

Odette looked from her mother to her godmother. "I was thinking of going there."

"*Mon Dieu!* Why?" her mother exclaimed. "You cannot confront such a person."

"It was just a thought," Odette said.

Bryan looked at her curiously. He had an inkling that she would do it and he hoped she would say why.

"If I could infiltrate his headquarters," she went on. "In a wig, sunglasses—maybe I could find out something that would put him out of business."

"And maybe you would get beat up or worse. Please do not play detective," her mother said sternly. "There is nothing to be gained. Hire someone if you want to waste your money. As your godmother says, Khong will simply go somewhere else."

Odette nodded, a little too quickly, Bryan thought. Uh-oh.

Jeanne didn't get there until well after midnight, looking as earnest and librarian-ish as Bryan remembered.

Good thing he hadn't actually seen her morph into the main attraction in the Vendredi's gender-bending revue. He didn't even want to think about it. She and Odette exchanged air kisses, and then Jeanne played detective for real.

She started with Lucie's computer, working in the cubicle without disturbing the mess in it. The assistant wasn't necessarily the only culprit but she sure as hell was the main suspect. But Khong's address was nowhere to be found on Lucie's computer.

No, the assistant had most likely done her dirty deal the old-fashioned way: in writing.

But something that might be related to the ever-expanding mess came up in her browser history anyway, based on the first five letters. Khongaroo Kids of Kansas.

Jeanne pulled up a website with a cute cartoon kangaroo boinging all over it. "*Merde.* I hate stupid Flash animation," she grumbled. "It takes forever to download and what is the point?" She clicked several keys in rapid succession. "I can't escape this ridiculous kangaroo!"

Odette looked over Jeanne's shoulder and studied the cartoon. When it stopped boinging, she clicked on the pouch. The site opened up.

"Why are you paying me?" Jeanne asked her.

"Because you know what you are doing."

"Hah." She scrolled around. "Kiddie pajamas. Animal sneakers. I don't think this is the fellow that paid Lucie to steal from you."

"Look a little longer."

"All right," Jeanne sighed. "I am almost too sleepy to be doing this." She took her time to trace several ISPs and came up with the address of the company. "Aha. It says it's based in Kansas but it only sells goods online and the office is in New York. Odette, do you remember the address that was on the paper in Lucie's bag? Come and look."

Odette looked over Jeanne's shoulder, and so did Bryan. "It must be right next door," they said in unison.

"A hop, skip, and a jump away," Bryan added. "It's an American expression."

The other two gave him a baffled look. "Okay, whatever," Jeanne said. "Now we find out who Lucie e-mailed most. *Cherchez l'homme.*"

She fooled around with the Find function, combing through Lucie's inbox. One name came up by the hundreds, incoming and outgoing: Brad Quinn.

"It is an American name, no?" Jeanne asked Bryan. "The English do not name their boys Brad."

"Could be."

Jeanne hummed under her breath as she went to other websites. "We will try the American bad-guy search sites first." She typed in the name as Bryan looked over her shoulder at the site. *HE SAID WHAT?* appeared in big, dancing letters meant to convey that snooping on your new man was going to be a blast. The site had to be thriving—some big companies had banner ads on it.

Bryan hoped no one had posted about him, doing a fast mental run-through of his better qualities. He was a nice, brainy, fit guy who did his utmost to please in bed and out, respected his girlfriend's moms *and* his girlfriends, put the lid down and kept his feet off the newer furniture.

Then he got focused. The website known as www.hesaidwhat.com was new to him, but this Brad Quinn was all over it. Actually, there were several.

He read the comments as Jeanne scrolled through.

"I think that must be the one," Jeanne said, pointing a finger at the screen. "A junior banker, based in France. Not a wizard of finance, evidently. This girl calls him Overdrawn. And that one calls him Short Stuff." The computer expert snickered at some of the other, much less polite comments.

Odette sighed. "It is as Madame Arelquin said. The ones closest to me seem to be to blame."

"We still have to deal with the Khong guy somehow. Now what? Report him to Interpol?"

"Not without proof." She waved a hand at Lucie's monitor. "This means nothing. We have confirmed our suspicions and I will find a reason to fire Lucie. Jeanne, please install keystroke-capturing software. She has another week. Perhaps she will lead us to other miscreants."

"*Oui*, Madame Gaillard," Jeanne said. The monitor reflected in her glasses as she got busy with that.

12

The jet screamed down to the JFK runway and landed with a bump.

"Wake up," Brian said softly to Odette. Even in two side-by-side first class seats, she was all over him.

She'd slept through the morning coffee and croissant service, which he'd managed to consume with one hand. He brushed the croissant crumbs off her.

"*Mon Dieu*," she muttered, running a hand through her hair. "I must look a fright."

"You look fierce. Hair like that has to be all the rage in New York."

"Marc says that fierce is good." She reached into the small personal organizer she'd stuffed into the seat pocket in front of her and found a mirror. Her eyes widened in horror at the sight of her reflection. "He is wrong. Fierce is fierce."

The pilot made an announcement about waiting for a gate.

"You have time to fix yourself up."

Odette did the best she could, combing her hair and putting on a touch of makeup.

Navy blue skirts stretched over narrow hips, the flight attendants stalked through the aisles like herons, collecting newspapers and casting curious looks at Odette.

"Are you Madame Gaillard?" one of them murmured, bending over. "*The* Madame Gaillard?"

"Ah—"

"I thought it was you. Are you in New York to give a show?"

"No. Please forgive me—I only just woke up," Odette said politely.

"Of course. My apologies. I just wanted to say that I wear only Oh! Oh! Odette!" the attendant whispered and winked at her.

For a second Bryan thought she was going to pull up her navy blue skirt and confirm the good news. But she rose when another attendant called to her.

"Excuse me," she said to both of them and hurried off.

"Ah, the price of fame," Odette said. "Do you mind? At least the other passengers are pretending not to notice us."

"I don't care. Let's not talk about it."

"They were looking at you."

"It's a free country. I guess I can handle getting looked at."

She sighed and stuck all her cosmetics back in her bag. "I do not like it once I am out of Paris. I wonder if I have time to pee. We are just sitting here not moving."

"They would probably roll out a red carpet to the toilet for you."

She patted his cheek as she undid her seat belt. "Very funny. But I must go."

She rose stiffly and took care of that, then plopped down beside him again. "Have we advanced in line?"

"Not an inch."

"The New York airports always have delays," she sighed.

"I wouldn't know," he reminded her. "It's my first trip to the East Coast and I had to complicate things by going all the way to Paris and then here. Next time I'll fly direct from LA. Thanks for paying my way, though."

"Thanks for not objecting. It is all the same money, anyway. It goes around and around the world, and rains where it wants to."

"Tell me again how you managed to make millions?"

"Not now." She was yawning hugely. "I wish I could go back to sleep. But then I will mess up my lipstick if I do."

"Put on your sunglasses."

Odette nestled into his shoulder. "I will."

The plane gave a lurch and they started rolling. But it was another hour before they disembarked and headed for customs, where Odette had to stop to pet Sniffy, the luggage-inspecting beagle, even though Sniffy was working, then on to the baggage claim.

She slipped on her sunglasses along the way. There stood their driver, among a crowd of others, holding a sign that said GAILLARD in large block letters.

"So much for traveling incognito," she said with a sigh.

Bryan looked around. "No photographers on this end. I think we're safe."

They said hello to the man, who didn't seem to speak much English or French. He was from Eastern Europe, Bryan judged after a glance at his limo license. He got them settled in the back of an immense town car, and Odette relaxed against the seat cushions.

"So squooshy. So American. I love town cars," she said.

Bryan thought of his wheels, a beater car now on its last legs, so to speak, and didn't answer. He was more impressed by the skyline in the distance.

He'd seen it from the window of the plane, a choppy line of

skyscrapers that looked to be all one color from JFK. In the car, as they got closer to Manhattan and the morning haze lifted, the buildings seemed much more different from one another and the city seemed to grow before his eyes.

There was something vital but also brutal about it. It didn't have the venerable charm of Paris and the looming tall buildings were kind of oppressive.

"Interesting, no?"

"If you like big cities."

"It is different when you are walking around. The inhabitants of New York can be very nice."

"I'll take your word for it." Bryan looked out at the skyline again, just before the town car went through a purple E-ZPass tollbooth and got sucked into a tunnel.

He breathed a little easier when that was over, feeling like a hick. But tunnels that went under rivers were just not his thing.

"Where are we?" he asked.

"In midtown. On the east side of Manhattan. Our hotel is on the west, not too far from the garment district."

The driver honked his way through the crowded streets, going down a one-way and around to get them there.

Guys shoving big metal racks crammed with dresses and bolts of material crowded the streets.

"Not what it once was," Odette was saying, "but I love to wander here." She tapped on the plastic partition when she recognized the hotel, paying the fare and tipping the brass-buttoned guy who came out with a luggage rack.

She seemed so used to this chaos. Bryan told himself it was no big deal. But he was grateful when they were alone in their hotel room at last.

He flopped on the bed. "I don't care if I never get on a transatlantic flight again. Whew. I'm done in."

"We can unwind tonight. Go to a show."

"No. Sleep," he mumbled, rolling over and grabbing a pillow.

"You big baby," she scolded him.

"You slept, Odette. On me. All the way from DeGaulle. Meaning I didn't."

"Ah, you poor thing."

Bryan sat up a little and removed the foil-wrapped mint pressed into his hair. Fortunately, none of the goo inside had been squeezed out. He put it on the night table, along with another one from the other pillow where she would lay her head. If she ever stopped talking.

"Mints on the pillow. Minty-fresh toothpaste in the WC. That must be why the room cost a mint," Odette giggled. "That too is an American expression, no?"

"Yes," he said, feeling deeply ashamed that she'd paid his fare to New York. At least he'd managed to finagle a connection to California, by abject begging and waving his original return trip ticket for an ultra-discount-economy-strapped-to-the-wing three-stop that ultimately ended at a small local airport near Newport Beach.

It had been the most interesting week of his life, but he couldn't keep up this pace and he did have a life that didn't involve fashion. Had never involved fashion.

He watched her unpack, pulling out various outfits and hanging them out.

Then, from a poufy-looking bag, she took out a short blond wig, going to the mirror to pull it on over her dark hair.

"How kinky."

"This is for tomorrow."

"Why?" He rolled over, intrigued by the transformation in her appearance. "I like the punk pixie look on you."

She inspected her reflection and then dug around in her makeup bag, taking out a tube of eyeliner, which she applied in wicked swoops to each of her eyelids. A slash of pale lipstick and she was done.

"Huh. So far, so good. I really like it."

"Nothing doing. This is for business."

"What kind of business, Odette?"

"The risky kind."

He got up and put his arms around her. "We're getting good at that. And I love the idea of having two different women in one night, especially when both of them are you."

She elbowed her way out of his embrace. "Not now. This wig makes my head ache."

He found out why she'd brought the blond wig soon enough.

They were walking up 39th Street and crossed at Seventh Avenue.

"There is the giant button," she said, scrabbling in her purse for sunglasses.

"Huh?" He looked up, distracted by the roaring traffic, not wanting to be run over by a taxi driven by a homicidal maniac.

Sure enough, there was a giant button, about fifteen feet high, leaning at an angle with a giant needle thrust through it.

"You are in the garment district," she said, sticking the sunglasses on her face. "Home of the garmentos. There goes one now."

A youngish guy with slicked-back hair and a sharp suit who was screaming orders into a cell phone shoved past them.

"Can you feel the magic?" Odette asked Byran.

He looked down at the trash on the sidewalk and took in the general grimness of this not-yet-gentrified part of Manhattan. "Not really."

"I wish I could say it gets better. It is interesting, though."

"Yeah, I could see why you'd say that."

He glanced at loft windows crammed with bolts of fabric and shops that sold things like buttons and trimmings and lace. Odette could probably spend days here.

She took his hand when the light turned green, and they went into a building that had been something special in the glory days of Art Deco.

Now it was shabby, the stairs to the elevators kicked and stomped on by thousands of—what had she called that guy? A garmento. He wondered if the feminine form was garmenta and then he wondered if it was an Italian word.

The bell dinged. An ancient man in a brass-buttoned uniform that looked too big for him drew open an accordion-style gate when the elevator slid open. He nodded without saying a word.

Jesus. Bryan had never seen an elevator like this, let alone a uniformed attendant.

He tried not to gawk.

"Khongaroo Kids, please," Odette said.

The elevator man nodded and pushed a brass lever over a half-circle to send them up, then reversed the motion to stop.

They thanked him and stepped out, heading down a hall lined with lumpy carpet. He stumbled over a lump. "I hope that wasn't a rat."

"Me too." Then Odette stopped. "Here we are. Ready?"

He beat on his sweater-covered chest. He'd worn the thickest one he had, (a) because New York in April was colder than Paris in April, and (b) so he would look bigger. Not that he wasn't built, but he was supposed to protect her, in case things got ugly with the kiddy-pajamas guy.

Odette tried the knob and went in, talking immediately to the receptionist. Bryan checked out the photos of apple-cheeked tots in budget sleepwear. It was hard to believe that her naughty, elegant designs had somehow ended up here.

The receptionist called someone in an inner office and then waved them toward a glass-paned door.

He was expecting to see thousands of seamstresses bent over sewing machines. Instead he saw the usual maze of cubicles, with various people studiously ignoring them and trying to seem invisible.

"I thought this place made children's sleepwear," he whispered.

"Everything is made abroad where labor is cheap," she whispered back. "This is a front office, that is all."

They paused outside another glass-paned door that had King Khong Enterprises on it in gold letters etched with black.

"Here I go," Odette said in a soft voice.

"No," he corrected her. "Here we go. But you can go first. I'm just the muscle."

Mr. Khong turned out to be a mild-mannered Asian guy with an accent Bryan couldn't place. Whatever. There was nothing memorable about him.

Odette got right to the point. She sat down, whipped off her sunglasses and stared Khong right in the eye. Then she crossed her legs and leaned forward.

He didn't blink. He didn't look down. The womanly weapons move of showing leg and boobs didn't seem to have any effect on him at all.

Bryan stood there observing the two of them, not at all sure how this game of cat-and-mouse worked. Or even which one was the cat and which was the mouse. He stuck his hands in his pockets and waited.

Odette made a big show of carefully folding her sunglasses and then unzipping her purse.

Really slowly.

As slowly as a stripper unzipped her g-string.

Bryan saw the thick wads of cash stuffed inside it.

Khong blinked. He'd seen them too.

"Mr. Khong," she said sweetly. "I represent the designer whose panties you stole."

"I beg your pardon?" Khong said.

Bryan hid a smile with a cough into his hand. Buttoned-down and proper, the dude definitely didn't look like the underwear-snatching type. But he was, in his way.

"You know what I mean." Odette gave Khong a stare that would have wilted a lesser man. "And I am prepared to make you an offer."

Khong touched his tie as if he wanted to loosen it, then let his hand drop to the table. "You can't steal an idea," he said. "Ideas are like—like flower petals. They float through the air."

"Exactly." She patted the bag of cash before zipping it back up, not so slowly. "And there is money to be made in petals, no?"

He harrumphed.

"My boss, Odette Gaillard, would like to produce an inexpensive line with you if the panties can be made right."

"Our production standards are the highest in our price range—" he began.

"I mean no sweatshops, Mr. Khong."

He looked uncomfortable again.

"Independent monitoring of workplace conditions."

"That adds to costs."

Odette gave him a big smile. "Of course. Inexpensive is a relative term. For a couturier looking to break into mass market licensing, the goods will carry a certain cachet. And a somewhat higher price tag than, say, Fruit of the Zoom."

"Loom," Bryan whispered. "Fruit of the Loom."

"Whatever. Do you understand what I am saying, Mr. Khong?"

He inclined his head.

"Then someone from Gaillard will contact you." She slid

her business card across the desk. "Perhaps even Odette her-self."

Mr. Khong nodded and rose, since she had risen. The good-byes were wary, and Bryan noticed that he kept looking at the purse filled with cash.

They didn't say a word as they walked down the hall and took the stairs instead of the elevator. Two at a time. Galloping with glee.

They ran out and across the street, ducking between the giant button and its needle to get to the next corner. Odette hailed a taxi and one came quickly.

"Fifth Avenue and 57th, please."

"Now what? Where are we going?"

"To the most glamorous store in New York."

"Is that what all that money is for?"

Odette laughed. "It worked on Khong. But I wasn't going to give it to him. I just wanted to get his attention."

"I think you did. So what happens next?"

"Who knows?" She looked out at the New York streets and the jumble of buildings, coffee carts, and table vendors. "He might do very well and I did want to launch a line that every woman can afford. If you can't beat them up, join with them."

"That's not quite how it goes, but I think I like your version better."

She rapped on the plexiglass partition.

"Hey, isn't that Tiffany's?" The blocky building and its small, deep-set windows was on their left.

"Yes. And Bergdorf Goodman is in back of us. And here is our final destination, a block away. Henri Bendel."

She flung a twenty at the cabdriver without asking for a re-ceipt, and jumped out. Then Bryan did, not quite as fast.

He looked up, feeling like a tourist. But then she was looking up too. The old, Beaux-Arts building with its high windows and sloped roof looked almost exactly like her atelier.

"I can see why you like this place," he said.

She hoisted her sack of cash. "They like me." Odette led the way inside.

13

One year later, in Paris...

Bryan stood in the wings as the bride was made ready, staring out over the heads of the assistants who circled her.

Fitted perfectly into a low bodice, her long skirt of silk chiffon floated around her like an ethereal cloud. The sleeves just barely covered her shoulders. An impossibly large pearl hung in the hollow at the base of her slender neck, suspended from an antique pendant mounting set with diamonds in white gold.

Her earrings were also pendant pearls, and her dark hair was swept up into a pearl-banded high chignon, covered by a floor-length veil.

The gems had been loaned for the occasion by Frederique & Baudelaire, and so had a couple of big brutes to guard them. They watched the proceedings impassively, standing like pillars of uniformed muscle behind the bride.

The crowd would go wild when she finished her walk, did her turn . . . and opened the dress in front and showed off underwear that would drive any groom out of his mind.

Odette had outdone herself. The set was one of a kind, the only one in the world. She'd modeled the bridal underthings for Bryan last night. Handmade white lace of incomparable fineness that had taken fifteen women a whole year to make. The pieces had come off the pins and bobbins only a week ago, fashioned into a fantasy bra and panty set. The opposite of her usual black and on her, not innocent at all.

He hadn't been allowed to touch them. But seeing her slide out of them and stand before him, more beautiful naked than dressed, was still a sublime experience.

She came up behind him and edged past, talking to the stylist and makeup artist who followed her.

"Is everything ready?" she asked.

"*Oui*," they replied in unison.

The three of them stopped in front of the model, who shifted a little to allow them to look at her from the front, side, and in profile.

Odette nodded.

She walked with the model to the parting in the curtain and turned to smile at Bryan as the model stepped out and thunderous applause began.

He went to her and put his arms around her waist. "The best for last, Odette."

"This show will be my last."

"Until you get bored and start designing again."

She made a face. "I suppose it could happen. One should never say never. But I do think I will like just being with you for a while. Anonymous and happy. And far away from Paris and the business."

"Think we'll make the flight to California?"

"With a little luck."

"We're running late. The traffic on the Champs-Élysées won't stop just because I'm in love with you."

Odette looked up, her eyes bright. "I still cannot quite believe it."

He took her hand and kissed it.

"Believe it. You're going to be mine. And there's been a new development. I'm talking about a lifetime."

"What? Bryan, last night you said you were not sure. That we should wait." She pouted. "I didn't care—"

"I stayed awake. I thought about it all night while you were sleeping in my arms. Couldn't think of a reason to wait, couldn't think of anything but how happy you made me. You were so busy this morning I didn't get a chance. But I have you where I want you now." He took her into his arms for a kiss that made her bend backwards and forget where she was.

Bryan was into it, not minding if anyone saw. No one did, not really, rushing past the lovers to get a peek at the grand finale. He and Odette could have been invisible. A small mob was gathered behind the curtain, looking at the bride on the runway.

The model was supposed to make a graceful curtsey at the end, then turn around to reveal the length and fineness of her train, and then . . . take it all off. Then Odette would step forth and take her final bow.

The crowd began to applaud and shout in raucous rhythm. The bride got down to the lace and nothing but the lace.

Odette straightened up with a sigh of pleasure. "Do it again," she murmured.

"Kiss you or tell you that I love you?"

"Kiss first."

He obliged. She surrendered.

"How about a ring to seal the deal?"

"Oh!" Her eyes widened with delight when he took the fine old rose-cut diamond ring she had admired out of his pocket.

"Ready?"

She stuck out her hand and closed her eyes. "Ready as I will ever be."

"I think that was you who said all that stuff about love being worth the risk. Just so we're on the same page about that, because I think so too."

"Yes." She was shaking. "That was me."

He slid it on and she stared at her hand with wonder. Then they got wrapped up in a kiss that could have gone on for days if someone hadn't pushed the button that dragged the curtains back.

Astonished, the audience saw Odette Gaillard kissing an unknown man whose hand was up her skirt. They went wild, stomping and giving yells of encouragement and calling for more. Camera flashes went off, fast pops of white-blue light that sparkled in their eyes.

Flustered, she smiled and waved at the shouting crowd. Bryan withdrew his hand and put his arm around her waist.

"Someone is taking pictures," he said through clenched teeth. "Here we go again. Khong is going to be livid if the exclusive designs for him are—"

"Our official photographer is taking them. Everyone's bag was searched. Smile. We are getting married!" she called to the audience.

"When?" someone called back.

Bryan took a deep breath. "As soon as the show is over."

"How romantic!"

He recognized the voice. It was Marc, smiling and clapping at the very end of the world, with Achille by his side.

"Well?" he asked Odette. "Are you ready to tell the world?"

"They already know!"

Turn the page for a preview
of Sharon Page's HOT SILK!

On sale now!

1

Before the start of the London Season, March of 1818

"The choice is yours, my love. I want you—you know that. Meet me tonight, in the gallery. Don't wear your gown. Wear something easy to remove . . ."

Grace Hamilton knew she should be scandalized by Lord Wesley's proposition. She should refuse. But she had been trying to stay strong and good and proper for a week and she could not resist any longer.

"I do not know, my lord," she whispered. He stood behind her, away from the hot, sparkling chandeliers and the swirling crowd, in the shadows of the ballroom at Collingsworth, ancestral home of the Marquis of Rydermere. Lord Wesley's home and a place she had no right to be.

Grace stood by dark gallery doors, wearing a borrowed gown, terrified everyone would see her for the fraud she was.

His lordship rested his hands gently on her waist, his long fingers splayed to meet across her middle—she hadn't expected him to touch her yet and the contact stole her breath. "I will be

237

waiting," he murmured, his voice a possessive growl. "If you aren't there at midnight, I will have to assuage my broken heart elsewhere."

How many other ladies here would accept his proposition? A wave of his hand and any number of women would beg to be kissed by him, would eagerly agree to meet him for sin. Dozens of women here wanted to marry him; their calculating eyes fixed on the prize—to become Marchioness of Rydermere.

This house teemed with lovely ladies of good birth, but Lord Wesley had singled her out, had pursued *her* ever since her arrival. From the first moment he had bent over her hand and let his lips play magic on her fingers through the thin muslin of her glove, she had been entranced. And each look he cast her way, each hot and intense glance, had assured her he felt the magic every bit as much as she.

Or was she wrong? What, after all, did she know about men in love?

"Midnight. By midnight," she teased, feigning a confidence she didn't feel, "you will know if I am coming or not."

His breath tickled her neck, a hot caress. "Wicked wench. I'll be there." He moved closer to her, leaving the shadows to press his body against hers. She both stiffened and melted as a hard ridge snuggled against her silk-clad bottom.

"I can't wait to grasp hold of this lush, fashionable arse—" With a groan, he ground his erection against her curves, setting her heart racing. "That, my golden nymph, is for you."

And then he was gone.

Grace snapped open her fan and beat it so feverishly the thin silk tore from the spokes. She'd never had a man do this to her before. Be so bold. Be so gruff and direct and lusty—

"What was my rascal of a brother saying to you? Oh, Grace, you aren't going to faint, are you? Your face is aflame."

Grace started guiltily as Lady Prudence joined her in the

private corner. Her friend's closed fan rested against her lips, half hiding their firm line. "Did you let him coax you here?"

"No . . . I needed a rest," Grace lied.

Lying had never been her talent and she doubted Lady Prudence was fooled. Her friend gave a tip to her head so the candlelight caught the tiny diamonds and sapphires threaded through her dark hair. Lady Prudence was so lovely. It was astonishing to Grace that she had such a friend.

"Don't believe a word he says," Lady Prudence warned, her gray-blue eyes very solemn. She bent close to be heard clearly over the graceful melody of the waltz. "My brother is a scoundrel."

Couples twirled past, elegant and glittering beneath the glow of a thousand candles. Gentlemen's hands rested lightly on slender backs; ladies' gloved hands entwined with those of their partners. Skirts swirled around graceful ankles and coattails fluttered to give glimpses of muscular male bottoms.

Grace sighed. "Aren't most of the men we encounter scoundrels at heart? That is what makes them so interesting. But no gentleman would ever really behave as a scoundrel with me."

"For which you should be profoundly grateful." They were the same age, both eighteen, but Lady Prudence suddenly looked wise and mature. "You are so exceptionally beautiful, Grace, you will make a devastatingly successful marriage."

"Will I?" She was running out of time. Within a week or two, the fashionable world would all be in London. Her eldest sister Venetia was already in London, in a rented townhouse, drawing erotic art to save their family, and their mother was sick with worry.

And Grace could save them all. All she had to do was marry.

She ground the toe of her slipper into the gleaming parquet floor and gripped her fan until the splintered spokes bit through her gloves. All she had to do was capture a titled man and she could keep her family from the workhouse. She could return her mother to the world that had cast her out.

Since Grace had turned thirteen, her plan had been direct and simple. She would marry a title. She would make things right. Everyone had told her she was lovely, that she would grow to be a great beauty. She had overheard the secret conversations, when matrons had told her mother how valuable her beauty would be.

"Grace, I am serious." Lady Prudence gripped her shoulders and gave her a gentle shake. The silk of Grace's gown—one of Lady Prudence's that she had bought but later decided she did not like—shimmered around her legs. "Do not believe a word my brother says," Lady Prudence warned. "There is not a young woman on this estate that he has not . . . had intimacies with."

"I know." And Grace did. She knew she was a fool to imagine that Lord Wesley, a wealthy heir, a devastatingly handsome man, would want to marry a nobody like her. But she knew, even after only a week, that she could not bear to settle for anything less. It was not his title she wanted—it was him. The man.

Grace tapped her lips with her torn fan. She wanted it all. Could she not only marry well, but also marry a man she loved and desired? Or was she simply hoping for too much, when her family's security was at stake?

Prudence had adopted a motherly air. "There are many gentlemen who are already besotted with you, Grace. Lord Ornsbrook, who is a viscount, and a wealthy one, is a thoroughly respectable catch. Pelworth hangs on your every word, and he is an earl!"

Grace swallowed hard. Either man should be perfect: young, reasonably attractive, and tongue-tied around her, which should be a good sign.

Prudence pointed with her fan at a lanky blond man laughing his way through the dance set. "Even Sir Randolph Thomas, over there. He possesses a fortune! Yes, he's an atrocious dancer, but, really, a woman never dances with her husband."

"Prudence, no—"

"Or Lord Wynsome. Such a suitable name. He melts every woman's heart. And he's heir to the Earl of Warren. He's delicious, isn't he? I'm certain he would take one look at you and—"

"Stop!" Grace cried. The Earl of Warren was her grandfather—her mother's father. He had thrown her mother out and barred all of them from his house. Lady Prudence, of course, knew not of that. Like everyone else, Prudence believed the lies Grace had carefully cultivated—the lie learned by her and her sisters. Her mother was respectably married, her father, a sea captain who was away, far across the world, hoping to make his fortune. But that father was her mother's fictitious creation.

She would never dare tell anyone that she was Lord Warren's illegitimate granddaughter and that her father was really Rodesson, the famous and scandalous artist of erotica. Or that her eldest and talented sister was the one now painting the erotic works that bore Rodesson's name.

Lord Wynsome had no idea she was, in fact, a cousin to him. There was no way he would guess, but it was still her greatest fear that he somehow would, that he would expose the truth to Lady Prudence.

Prudence was her entry to the ton, to the world of rich and titled and delicious gentlemen—

She couldn't dare risk Prudence's friendship. And, in truth, she dearly loved her friend.

"But, still, there are more," Prudence said cheerfully. "Over there—" She stopped abruptly. "Oh good heavens, what is he doing here?"

Grace never heard that tone of voice from Prudence. Low, serious . . . fearful. Surprised, she strained to look.

A gentleman stood at the entrance to the ballroom—he towered head and shoulders above the crowd. He must have been over six and a half feet in height. And his hair—it was a wild mane of dark blond that streamed past his shoulders, unruly and wild. She knew, by instinct, that it suited the man.

He gave an enormous grin, which revealed deep dimples framing his handsome mouth and brilliant white teeth. Several servants were trying to push him out. With his arms crossed over his huge chest, he appeared to be an immovable wall.

The butler hastened up to the fray, but the mysterious guest merely amiably punched the servant in the shoulder.

Laughing, openly amused, the gentleman refused to budge. To Grace's shock, she saw his head turn and his gaze slide over the crowd. Toward her. She was staring, but so was everyone else. There was no reason he should feel her curious gaze out of the hundreds of others.

Polite decorum decreed she should look away, but she could not stop watching him. His skin was golden bronze, close in color to his luxurious hair. He was obviously a man who exposed his body to the sun. Even bathed in the light of a chandelier, he stood too far away to reveal the color of those penetrating eyes, but she guessed they would be blue.

A silly fancy. She forced her gaze to move demurely away. But she was still aware of him; it was as though the music had stopped and the dancers had whirled away into the night, and there was no one in the ballroom but the handsome stranger and her.

The strangest sensation gripped her, along with a heat that threatened to set her skin on fire.

She'd desired Lord Wesley, but she'd felt nothing like this—

Every forbidden erotic picture, every one of her father Rodesson's erotic drawings—those she'd secretly looked at—spilled through her heated mind.

She wanted this man, this powerful, compelling stranger. She wanted to know what it would be like to lie underneath him and part her legs and take him inside her. She wanted to know how his skin would taste to her lips and her tongue. To know if he would be rigid and big and if he would fill her completely and make her scream in pleasure. She wanted to see him naked, taste him naked, and make love to him until they were both sweaty and senseless—

He was staring at her.

Grace felt it. Felt an answering fire rush over her skin.

Preposterous! How could he even see her? But she glanced up, enthralled by the moment, knowing their gazes would lock—

Or was he looking at Prudence? Wouldn't that make more sense?

He was not looking at either of them. Abruptly he turned on his heel and strode out through the gilt and ivory doors.

Her fan was in tatters beneath her fingers and her heart felt two sizes too big for her chest. Her throat was tight and dry. Her drawers were indecently wet.

She had to know. It was like a sudden addiction. "Who was that?" she cried.

"My half brother." Prudence's voice shook with . . . anger? Fear? An emotion Grace could not quite define.

"You have a half brother?"

"He's a bastard," Prudence continued, her voice contemptuous, using a word she should not. "My father's by-blow. His first-born child, in fact, and my father is stupidly fond of him."

Grace shook at the revulsion on her friend's face. She was a bastard. Would Prudence feel the same way about her if she knew the truth?

Suddenly Grace felt as though she stood on a tightrope, balancing over a pit of wolves. No, this was the ton. Not wolves— mocking jackals with slavering jaws.

"He should be hung," Prudence spat. "He's a highwayman. Can you believe he is so bold as to come to this house? He's probably robbed half the people here! And he was a pirate. Why the British Navy did not kill him, I cannot imagine. He's a murderer, a scoundrel, and . . ." Prudence took a shaky breath.

Grace moved forward, startled by tears in her friend's eyes.

"And our father loves him best!" Prudence cried and stamped her foot.

Grace hugged her friend. "Of course not!"

Prudence pulled out of the hug, shaking. "He does. His mother was a love affair, ours a duty marriage. Of course, he loves dashing Devlin Sharpe. But I *hate* him."

"Why? Because of what he is?" Grace could hardly believe she wanted to press this. Why should she want to hear about the horrors of being recognized as a bastard?

"He murdered the man I loved. If I wouldn't hang for it, I'd grab one of my father's pistols right now and shoot him where he stands."

Grace blinked. "How could he murder a man and escape punishment?"

Prudence balled her hands into fists, and Grace heard her fan snap. "I cannot tell you what happened. Not even you, my dear friend."

She reached out and stroked Prudence's arm as her friend turned red-rimmed eyes to her and asked, "Do I look awful? I have to dance with Lord Wynsome next."

"You look fine." But a chill washed over Grace as she watched Prudence stroll away. Prudence's movements were controlled, precise, and lovely, belying her emotional outburst. If her illegitimate half brother had murdered the man she loved, how could he have dared walk into the house?

And even after hearing what a beast he was, she still ached between her legs. She was still flushed and anxious with desire.

She was supposed to meet Lord Wesley at midnight . . . After feeling all that mad, delirious passion and hunger and need.

She couldn't bear to stand in this crowded, overheated ballroom one moment longer. She needed to escape.